Apache Thunder

Spotting a heavy strong-box being loaded onto a stage-coach, the notorious Mexican bandit Zococa and his mute Indian friend Tahoka decide to follow. The fact that the coach contained a beautiful female passenger was an added temptation that Zococa could not resist.

As the stage travelled through the usually peaceful Apache country, the Indians unexpectedly attacked. Lured by the strong box and the plight of an unknown woman with the pretty face, Zococa and Tahoka risk their lives and ride to the assistance of the beleaguered stagecoach.

Soon the incomparable pair find themselves embroiled in a deadly mystery that only their unique skills can untangle. Justice would be done!

Apache Thunder

ROY PATTERSON

A Black Horse Western

ROBERT HALE · LONDON

© Roy Patterson 2001
First published in Great Britain 2001

ISBN 0 7090 6966 9

Robert Hale Limited
Clerkenwell House
Clerkenwell Green
London EC1R 0HT

Typeset by
Derek Doyle & Associates, Liverpool.
Printed and bound in Great Britain by
Antony Rowe Limited, Wiltshire

Dedicated to Gary George

PROLOGUE

Luis Santiago Rodrigo Vallencio had sought and found the fame he had always desired. Somehow managing to create his own myth along the dry dusty trails which had haunted his life, he had become a living legend on both sides of the long sun-baked border which separated Texas and his homeland of Mexico.

He was a bandit unlike any other. He was loved by women and respected and feared by men; a man who had managed to exaggerate his own prowess as a bandit to such legendary levels that they bore little relation to reality and had earned him a price on his head. Dead or alive. Yet even this did nothing but amuse the always smiling man. He was proud of the fact that he was known as the greatest bandit of them all.

Yet few knew his real name.

To the masses he was the smiling one. The

brave one. The left-handed one. The one man upon whom you could rely to come to the aid of even the lowliest of souls and not ask for anything in return.

He was the bandit who rode with the silent giant called Tahoka, an Apache warrior whose life he had saved many years earlier.

Clad in black with a sombrero covered in silver thread he rode proudly upon his pinto stallion.

The name of Luis Santiago Rodrigo Vallencio might have been unknown . . . but everyone had heard tell of the bandit with the heart of gold.

Everyone knew the name of Zococa!

ONE

Mission Wells was a town like any other along the seemingly endless border, small and baked dry by a merciless sun. More Mexican than Texan in its appearance yet ruled by the laws of the Lone Star State, the town had found itself almost forgotten by everyone except the wealthy landowners on both sides of the border. Cowboys and *vaqueros* gathered in equal numbers most days after the sun had set. Saloons and cantinas seemed to burst to overflowing most evenings as the well-paid saddle kings spent their handsome wages on liquor and the company of friendly females.

Yet Mission Wells had one thing which set it apart from other small border towns; a very large bank swollen with the gold of its patrons. In the half-century that Mission Wells had existed, the bank had never been robbed. This too was something quite extraordinary considering the location of the town itself. The bank seemed extremely vulnerable, being so close to the Mexican border, yet no gang either of outlaws, or of bandits, had ever tried to breach its meagre defences.

Why? The explanation was simple. Although a dozen ranchers controlled the land encircling Mission Wells and used the vast ranges of endless land to raise their cattle, this was also the land of the Apache. Even if a gang of ambitious robbers had managed to hold up the bank, there simply was no safe route away from this place.

The most fertile lands were filled with the well-armed ranchers and their armies of cowboys. No outlaw gang would try to make their way through there. Everywhere else within a hundred square miles was like Mission Wells itself, dry and barren and home to thousands of migrating Apache.

To the north-west, on the edge of a vast parched desert, sand-coloured mountains concealed no fewer than four Apache tribal camps. This too was a place no sane white man would enter unless he had something to trade, buy or sell. This was an empty land where not only the skeletons of men and animals bleached in the sun, but buildings too. On the edge of the desert a few wooden poles still stood marking the spot where an army fort had died along with most of its occupants. Now only drifting sand moved within the once solid walls.

Even God had found this place beyond His ability to tame, as the deserted adobe structure at the very foot of the dry mountains testified. An entire mission had been built here a hundred years earlier amidst the high cactus, around a gentle creek which ran off the high peaks. Whoever had built the solid structure had worked hard. High walls surrounded six small dwellings and a larger building resembling a church. Yet only rattlers and cougars visited this place now.

Yet for all this land's hostility, a stage route had been established nearly ten years earlier and ran regularly between El Paso and Mission Wells. In all those ten years it too had remained unhindered by either outlaws or the Apache.

So it seemed that the bank at Mission Wells had stayed untouched because it appeared that there was nowhere safe to go if anyone dared to rob it.

Only death seemed to wait out beyond the boundaries of the small border town. There were a thousand ways this land could take life and destroy it. That was how it had always been and none of the town's citizens imagined it would alter in their lifetime.

They might have changed their minds had they realized who was approaching.

As the sun was setting across Mission Wells, two strangers rode towards the town's alluring lights.

The town was busy as usual as the street-lamps were being lit along the main thoroughfare. Tinny pianos and out-of-tune guitars began to haunt the streets with music as men from both sides of the border converged upon Mission Wells to spend the hours of darkness fruitfully.

As riders of every kind sought out the best saloons and gambling halls, the two strangers entered the town of Mission Wells unnoticed.

Using the shadows as their shield, the pair rode slowly along the busy main street towards their goal. The bank. Both had heard all the stories of how it was pointless robbing the bank because there was nowhere to go with the loot, but neither rider lived by other men's rules. To them, it was a challenge to try and break the rules. To do the impossible took daring and perhaps a little luck.

The leading horseman used just two fingers of his right hand to hold the reins of his tall pinto stallion. The palm of his left hand rested on the mother-of-pearl grip of the pistol on his left hip. He saw everything as he allowed the magnificent horse to walk slowly along the noisy streets. Nothing escaped the dark handsome eyes beneath the black sombrero laced with silver thread. For this was the man known as Zococa, the left-handed one.

Zococa, the most notorious bandit of them all. A man whose fame was mostly self-professed, but whose courage and accuracy with his pistol none had ever matched. A man who relished being famous because it made men fear him and women adore him. For Zococa, there could be no better life.

The second rider who guided his mount in the hoof-prints of the pinto stallion was decidedly different in appearance. Not only from the rider he followed, but from any other living man. He was huge by any standards. He was known as Tahoka. He was also the biggest Apache anyone had ever set eyes upon. Like his partner, he was a bandit but, unlike Zococa, he could not speak. Many years earlier the young Mexican had discovered Tahoka staked out over an ant-hill. Whoever had mutilated the huge Indian had done a good job. More dead than alive, Tahoka had had his tongue cut from his mouth and been tortured beyond most men's endurance. Robbed of his manhood, he somehow survived his injuries and remained with Zococa.

Why the two riders had found themselves at Mission Wells was in itself a mystery. Teasing a posse twenty miles south for over two hours, the pair had suddenly realized they could not return to their hideout in Mexico. Forced to ride across the great river just to outwit their pursuers, Zococa had recognized the small town nestling in the dry hills. He knew of its bank and the stories which had grown around this place: stories which tempted the vanity of the handsome bandit.

'Are we not short of funds, my little one?' Zococa had asked his friend when they first set eyes upon the painted sign which told them the name of the town before them.

The huge Apache brave had nodded in agreement.

'Is there not a very fat bank in Mission Wells?' Zococa had reasoned.

Tahoka had nodded in agreement again.

'Then is it not our duty to allow this bank to lose a little weight?' the smiling Mexican bandit had added. 'After all, who wants to see a fat ugly bank when they could look at a healthy slim one?'

Tahoka began to talk with his fingers and hands as he tried to convey the stories of how it was impossible to escape this place even if you were successful in robbing its bank.

'Quiet, my little rhinoceros. You give me the headache with your constant nagging. I know of the stories but that is all they are. Just stories to frighten the women and the little children.'

The huge Apache had tried to make his partner look at his hands as he continued to argue. It was a pointless exercise.

'We are brave bandits, *amigo*. We will rob the bank and we will find ourselves a safe haven. Do not fear, I have a plan.'

The expressionless Indian had shrugged and followed his talkative friend along the hot sandy trail towards the town as night had fallen.

Zococa did not stop talking until they reached the very edge of the small town. Only as his magnificent pinto stallion began to move between the buildings did the bandit close his mouth and become serious. Or as serious as it was possible for him to become.

If Zococa had one problem, it was his inability to take anything totally seriously. Even being wanted Dead or Alive seemed to make the young bandit proud rather than concerned. He had worked hard to create a reputation far exceeding his own true worth. For being a famous bandit was, to Zococa, something he knew made many females look kindly upon him. To have Zococa make love to you was far more glamorous than having an ordinary cowboy court you.

It was a dangerous game to play but the bandit thrilled at being chased either by posses of gunmen or by beautiful admiring women.

As Zococa allowed the stallion to walk through the shadows of the town, he listened to the sounds which echoed off the wood-and-adobe walls of its buildings, sounds which denoted by the mixture of accents and music that this was a border town. Hundreds of people with only one thing on their minds filled the night air with their laughter as they sought even a brief moment of happiness. Zococa had heard it all before in dozens of similar towns on either side of the border.

Zococa reined in his horse and waited a few seconds for his partner on his black mount to draw level with him. Both men stared at the large building with the word BANK painted on a wooden sign above its doorway.

'Is it not a nice little bank, Tahoka? Can you not hear all the money inside calling out to us?'

The Apache looked around the streets as people moved from building to building, totally unaware of the presence of the two bandits.

'Do you not think we might find much money in this place, my noisy one?' Zococa asked. He pulled out a long thin cigar and placed it between his perfect teeth. 'I think business will be good tonight.'

Tahoka continued staring around the town and the variety of its buildings as his companion struck a match and lit the cigar.

'You are not concentrating, Tahoka. Are you hungry?' Zococa asked as smoke drifted from his mouth.

The Apache nodded and patted his stomach.

'You have no head for the business, my little one. You do not understand the finer details of our work. We should rob the bank and then buy food.' Zococa felt his friend's strong hand grip his free arm before he turned to look at the huge Indian. 'You wish the food first and then we rob the bank?'

Tahoka nodded.

'Very well. We shall eat first.' Zococa sucked in hard on his cigar as his eyes searched for somewhere to eat. Then he saw a small cantina halfway down a dark street resonant with guitar music. Set amid a dozen other buildings, the cantina was almost identical to countless others to be found in every town in southern Texas. Kicking his spurs gently into the sides of his stallion, Zococa aimed the huge pinto at the cantina with his large friend riding at his side. The street was quieter than most of the others within the boundaries of Mission Wells mainly due to the fact it was the only one without a saloon or gambling hall. This suited the pair of riders.

Zococa and his hungry friend drew their mounts up outside the cantina and inhaled the overwhelming aroma of chilli. The bandits gazed up and down the dark, twisting, heavily scented thoroughfare before satisfying themselves its shadows held nothing to be wary of.

As Zococa dismounted and tied his reins to the branch of a rose bush, he paused and once more looked up and down the street, noting that this seemed the quietest part of Mission Wells. Most of the activity was centred around the saloons in the main street opposite the bank. To Zococa, this was perfect. He preferred to move around in the shadows of night, unnoticed by eyes which might become too curious. Too brave.

'I think we shall find good food here, *amigo.*' The words drifted in the smoke of Zococa's cigar as Tahoka marched quickly into the cantina leaving his companion alone in the dark, quiet street.

Zococa checked his pockets and pulled out a handful of gleaming silver dollars. The bandit looked at the coins in the palm of his hand thoughtfully. This represented their entire fortune, a mere six silver dollars. Gripping the cigar in his teeth, the tall bandit turned and pushed his way through the beaded curtain. As he stepped into the cantina, Zococa looked from beneath the brim of his black sombrero at the occupants of the warm room until the beads stopped swaying behind him. Seeing nothing to trouble him Zococa walked to where the mute Apache was seated.

The cantina seemed far quieter than Zococa thought it ought to as he removed his sombrero and dropped it on to an empty chair. He sat down next to the hungry Tahoka.

'It seems very quiet, Tahoka. Too quiet.' Zococa rested his left hand on the grip of his pistol, watching the faces of the few other customers as they, in turn, studied him and his unusual companion. The faces were Mexican and posed no threat.

Tahoka rested his elbows on top of the wooden table and pointed at the kitchen area where a large middle-aged woman seemed preoccupied with her cooking. Flames leapt into the air as the female expertly prepared her dishes.

'She is very broad but I like this in a woman,' Zococa said, studying the ample figure of the cook. 'I am very tired though, little one.'

Tahoka shook his head and pointed again, this time more earnestly.

'What?' Zococa asked. 'Why do you point your finger?'

The Apache warrior began to use his fingers to spell out what he meant to the handsome bandit.

Suddenly the eyes of the young bandit saw what the finger of his partner had been aiming at. A man sat in the shadows beyond the cooking range, next to an open doorway eating his supper. A man who wore a sheriff's star across his chest. A man who had not, as yet, noticed them.

As Tahoka began to rise from his chair to leave, Zococa placed a hand upon the man's arm and forced him down again.

'Do not panic. We are here to eat.'

Tahoka began to speak with his hands again. Zococa nodded as he read the silent words of his companion.

'He is only an *Americano*, my friend. Look at him eat. This is not a man of genius like myself,'

Zococa joked, trying to calm his large friend even though he could feel his own perspiration trickling down his neck.

It seemed an eternity before the cook turned and saw the two men seated and watching not only her but also the eating lawman. She was more attractive than either man had anticipated, despite her wide frame. She rubbed her hands upon her apron and walked towards them, smiling. Only when she reached the pair did she suddenly realize that her customers might be slightly different from her normal clientele.

'I have heard many tales of a handsome bandit who rides with a giant Apache warrior.' Her voice was sweet and low as she stood between them and the sheriff at the rear of the cantina.

'I have also heard these stories, my lovely one.' Zococa smiled as he stared up through his cigar smoke into the woman's concerned face. 'What is your name?'

'My name is Evita, *señor.*'

'A beautiful name for a beautiful lady.' Zococa smiled broadly as she moved closer.

'Are you Zococa, my flirtatious one?' she asked, trying to conceal her blushes from his prying eyes. Eyes which seemed to have the ability to stare through any woman's clothing until they found what they sought.

'*Sí*, this is what they call me,' Zococa admitted.

'Does this trouble you?'

'Have you not seen the sheriff eating, Zococa?' asked Evita's anxious voice.

'He seems to see nothing but the food on his plate.' Zococa leaned slightly to glance across the cantina at the man wearing the star on his vest.

Evita was worried. 'He is very mean. He is also very smart, Zococa. He will try to arrest you both when he sees you.'

Zococa grinned.

'Many have tried but so far nobody has been successful.'

'You must flee, my brave one,' she urged.

'But we are hungry, Evita,' Zococa protested. 'My friend is shrinking from hunger before my eyes.'

The woman used her wide body to conceal her notorious customers from the eyes of the sheriff as she tried to think of a solution to her problem. She wanted no blood spilled in her cantina.

'Quickly, Zococa. Take your friend up the stairs behind you to the first room on the right. You shall be safe there until the sheriff has finished eating and gone.'

Zococa rose to his feet, picked up his sombrero and moved his head for his partner to follow him. Tahoka stood and pointed to his belly and then his mouth.

'Tahoka is very hungry, my lovely one.' Zococa

touched Evita's soft cheek with his lips before turning to face the tiled steps which led to the upper level.

'I shall have Zena my daughter bring food up for you both in a few minutes,' the woman said.

'Daughter! Is she beautiful?' Zococa paused as his imagination began to race.

'*Sí*. She is also only seven years old, Zococa,' the smiling woman added.

As the two bandits quickly ascended the stairs, Zococa looked at his huge friend. 'Seven years old. Did I not tell you we rode far too quickly? I think we arrived at this cantina about nine years too soon, *amigo*.'

TWO

The Overland Stage Company had controlled the long-distance stage routes that fringed the Texas–Mexico border for over ten years. They made their profits from linking remote towns and cities where none of the larger stage companies cared to operate. Another reason for the success of the Overland, was that they operated their stage-coaches in remote regions where it would prove too expensive or dangerous for train companies to lay track.

Most of the stagecoach companies had seen their monopoly of transporting passengers across the West disappear on the safer direct trails between the main towns and cities with the coming of the iron horse. Yet out in the still-hostile terrain along the sun-baked desert plains, stagecoach travel was still a viable operation.

The Overland Stage Company had carved out a niche for itself along the border over the preceding decade by building a series of small outposts called way stations. These providers of fresh mounts and hot food, spread throughout the remote prairies, allowed the stages to change teams and themselves to make a little extra money from the captive passengers by selling them hard liquor. Even the most upstanding of souls could find themselves indulging in the odd glass of whiskey, after having their bones shaken loose in the cramped confines of a stagecoach.

As midnight resounded around Mission Wells, the office manager seemed less than happy as he studied the six-horse team being backed into the wooden traces of the stagecoach. Leaning against the wall of the office, Griff Drake had been brooding over news which had arrived a few hours earlier.

Drake had been informed by the distressed driver of the earlier south-bound stage that the Apaches in the mountains that towered over the trail had been spotted watching the narrow pass.

For a tribe who were seldom seen, the appearance of a few dozen braves perched high above the only route in and out of Mission Wells from the north was cause for concern.

They had never had any trouble with the Apaches before but the driver had been scared. Real scared.

Drake chewed on the stem of his pipe as he

watched the white-haired driver approaching the office from the direction of the saloons. It was hard to tell whether old Salty Sagebrush had been drinking, since he always had the look of a man who had just awoken from a long sleep. Yet in reality, there were few keener or more capable men in all of Texas.

Sagebrush had no teeth and sported a wild beard which matched his unkempt mane of hair. When he spoke, folks tended to listen hard, mainly due to the way he slaughtered practically every word which dripped off his long tongue.

'Get in here, Salty. You're late, as usual,' Drake said as he moved into the office holding his clipboard in his nervous shaking hands.

The old-timer followed the sweating man up to a desk covered in papers. Sagebrush immediately knew that Griff Drake was worried about something, and had a fair idea what that something was.

'I don't like it, Griff. Nope, I'm a leetle bit worried, and that's the truth. There's Apaches up in the pass and I gotta drive that stagecoach right under their long noses.'

Drake pulled a half-bottle of whiskey from a shelf together with two glass tumblers which he filled. 'Shut up and drink, you old fool.'

Sagebrush lifted the glass up and inhaled the fumes before throwing the amber liquid into his mouth and swallowing. His tongue seemed to suddenly emerge and rotate over his facial hair, lapping up any of the whiskey which might not have made it into the gaping cavity which was his toothless mouth.

'That's a nice drop, Griff.'

Drake sipped at his whiskey and watched the old driver filling his glass again, then resting his hip on the edge of the desk. Salty Sagebrush might not have won many beauty contests but he sure knew everything there was to know about anything with four wheels. In his case, looks were definitely deceptive.

'I guess you heard about the Apache over in the saloon?' Drake sighed heavily.

'Yep. I heard.' Sagebrush downed the second glass of whiskey before moving to the gun-rack on the wall and studying the line of twenty Winchesters laced together with a sturdy chain.

'What you reckon?' Drake asked the wily old man. 'Am I just showing my inexperience by being worried?'

Sagebrush nodded. 'You can't help being a leetle bit of a greenhorn, Griff. Ain't your fault.'

'You figure you'll need extra weaponry?' Drake asked.

'I reckon I needs me a few of these carbines and a couple of boxes of cartridges, Griff,' Sagebrush replied, stroking his white chin-hair thoughtfully.

26

Drake moved to the side of the shorter man.

'How come you need three rifles?'

Sagebrush's eyes sparkled in the light of the oil-lanterns as he faced the manager. 'Just in case, Griff. Just in case.'

'Just in case of what?'

'You ever seen a bunch of Apaches when they gets their dander up, boy?' Sagebrush asked. He strolled to the small window which looked into the waiting-room.

Griff Drake lifted a heavy key-chain off the table and began searching for the key that would release the padlock from the chain which was woven through the trigger guards of the deadly weaponry. At last he found it.

'But why do you want three rifles?' Drake repeated his question as the chain fell heavily to the floor. 'Surely one would do?'

'I might need some of these passengers to help me and Josh, Griff.' The old man rubbed the glass window, allowing a clearer picture of the waiting passengers in the dimly illuminated room next to the office. What he saw gave him little heart.

Within the cramped confines of the waiting-room only two figures waited patiently. The first was a handsome female wearing dark clothing and a hat. At her side she had a small bag. Seated on the opposite side of the room was a man dressed in military dress-uniform. He was probably in his late fifties, judging by the white mutton-chop whiskers which protruded from beneath his black hat.

'Who are they, Griff?' Sagebrush asked, wondering how much use either of them might be should he drive the stage into trouble.

Drake lowered the three Winchesters on to the table, sending a pile of papers cascading to the floor.

'The pretty one is a Miss Clara King. Leastways, that's what she calls herself. '

Sagebrush licked his lips. 'A single woman, huh? Could be my lucky day.'

Drake opened the top right-hand drawer of his desk and pulled out two boxes of carbine shells.

'She can't be no more than twenty, Salty.'

Sagebrush winked. 'A tad older than I'm used to but if she gets a leetle big romantic, I ain't gonna stop her. I draws women like flies to a butcher shop.'

Drake sat down in his chair. 'The old soldier is Major Lincoln. He's on his way to El Paso.'

Sagebrush walked across the room and looked out at the noisy buildings opposite. Mission Wells was enjoying itself into the early hours as usual.

'Is that the only passengers? Seems hardly worth the risk for just two.'

Drake struck a match, rested the flame on the bowl of his pipe and sucked in the smoke.

'You got one more passenger and a very important cargo, Salty.'

Sagebrush turned and screwed up his eyes as he tried to see through the dense pipe-smoke. 'One more? Who?'

'Judge Holmes,' Drake answered. He moved the pipe to the corner of his mouth and continued puffing nervously.

'Old Holmes the banker?' Sagebrush seemed interested at the thought of transporting his least favourite man.

'Yep. The banker.'

'Where is he?' Sagebrush cast a look out of the office up and down the street, trying to locate the man he knew only too well.

'You have to pick him and a money-box up from the bank before starting out for El Paso,' Drake said. He lowered the pipe and held it in his right hand.

'How come?' Sagebrush was curious.

'The money-box is mighty heavy.'

'How come he's taking a money-box to El Paso?' Sagebrush asked, staring through his thick white eyebrows.

'I only sell the tickets, Salty. I ain't in the confidence of folks like Holmes.' Drake spat at the floor as he noticed the older man looking as if he had seen something important.

Sagebrush straightened up as the burly young

figure of Josh Willis headed towards the office.

'I see my guard has finally dragged himself away from that wife of his, Griff.'

'About time,' Drake said.

'Mind you, if'n I had me a wife that looked like Josh's, I might be a tad reluctant to leave home too.' Sagebrush winked knowingly.

Drake stood as the muscular man stepped up on to the boardwalk and entered the office. The floor seemed to groan under his weight.

'Take these Winchesters and put them up in the driver's box, Josh. Take the cartridge-boxes too.'

Willis was a man of few words and simply grunted as he did as he was instructed.

Drake walked around his desk to the door and rested a hand upon the thin shoulder of the old man.

'Keep your eyes wide open on this trip, Salty. I can't afford to lose my best driver.'

Sagebrush smiled with his wrinkled eyes.

'Shucks, Griff. Them old Apaches ain't gonna start no trouble with Salty Sagebrush Esquire.'

THREE

Just as Zococa and Tahoka were about to ride out of the shadows, they heard the sound of the stage-coach approaching. Both riders reined in their mounts and sat in their saddles opposite the bank. They allowed the shadows to drape over them as the six-horse team galloped noisily towards them down the street from the offices of the Overland Stage Company.

Both bandits watched as, to their surprise, the driver halted the large vehicle outside the impressive bank. Zococa steadied his mount as he caught sight of a gleam of lantern-light escaping from the doorway of the building. The two riders watched the bank's door open and a small figure wave to the stagecoach guard. Josh Willis climbed down from his lofty perch and made his way towards Judge Holmes.

Zococa rubbed his chin with his slim index finger.

'This is most interesting, little one,' he whispered to the large Apache brave. 'I wonder why the stagecoach guard is going to the bank at this unholy hour.'

Tahoka nodded thoughtfully as he watched the burly Josh Willis heave up the strongbox and carry it to the waiting coach.

'I think there must be money in that box, Tahoka.' Zococa smiled at his partner.

Josh Willis used every ounce of his strength to lift the metal box up to the driver's seat, then he allowed it to fall beneath where Sagebrush sat holding the heavy reins in his hands and resting one foot on the long brake-pole.

Judge Holmes locked the door of the bank and then rushed to the stage. He pulled the door open, climbed in and sat next to Major Lincoln.

'This is most interesting, is it not?' Zococa gripped his reins tightly and ignored the sight of Willis climbing up to sit next to the driver. All the bandit could see was the face of the attractive Clara King who sat next to the window, opposite her two fellow passengers. 'Most interesting.'

Tahoka gave his friend a glance. He could sense by the tone of Zococa's voice that he had been distracted from their original plan.

Sagebrush allowed the brake-pole to spring back and slapped the reins of the six-horse team. He drove the vehicle along the well-lit streets until he finally left the town.

Tahoka began to use his hands to speak to his companion.

'Quiet, *amigo*. I think I have a better plan,' Zococa said. He allowed his pinto to stride out into the street. 'I think we shall not rob the bank but maybe follow the stagecoach with the most beautiful lady inside.'

Tahoka used his hands again to talk.

Zococa watched his partner's hands before speaking again. '*Sí, amigo*. We will rob the stagecoach eventually. But is it not amusing to think that I may be able to make love to such a divine creature first?'

Both bandits rode down the long street until they reached the offices of the Overland Stage Company where Griff Drake was locking up the doors for the night, ready to go home. He heard the two riders slowing their mounts to a halt behind him and turned to look in their direction.

'*Señor*, could you please tell my little friend and myself where the stage is heading?' Zococa asked.

Drake felt the hairs on the nape of his neck standing on end as he faced the two riders.

'El Paso. It's heading for El Paso.'

'And is the beautiful lady inside the stage going all the way to El Paso?' Zococa asked.

'Yep.' Drake replied fearfully.

'And her name, *señor*?'

33

'Miss Clara King.' Drake felt his mouth go dry as he uttered the name of the young female passenger. His mind raced as he stared up at the two horsemen. The stone-faced Apache simply sat watching him coldly whilst the handsome Mexican smiled continuously as he spoke.

'Miss Clara King? She is unmarried? This is very good fortune for me, I think.' Zococa grinned in hopeful anticipation.

'Who are you, mister?' Drake asked.

'A villain, *amigo*. Just a villain who has been hit by Cupid's arrow.' Zococa smiled amiably.

Griff Drake felt sweat running down between his shoulder-blades. 'I ain't too sure whether you're serious or just pulling my leg.'

'I have never been to El Paso. Quickly, Tahoka, we ride.' Zococa smiled and allowed the mighty pinto stallion to rear up and kick at the air. Then he hauled his reins hard to his right and spurred his mount into action. The two riders thundered through the streets in the direction taken by the stagecoach.

'Who was that, Griff?' Sheriff Bob Lane asked as he approached the confused Drake from across the wide street.

Griff Drake watched open-mouthed as Zococa and Tahoka disappeared from sight. The lawman stepped up on to the boardwalk beside him.

'I ain't sure, Bob.'

'The one on the pinto looked like a real fancy Mexican to me,' Lane said. He used a toothpick on his teeth. 'I couldn't make out the other rider.'

'He was an Indian,' Drake said thoughtfully.

'An Indian?'

'The biggest damn Indian I ever set eyes upon,' Drake added.

The sheriff grabbed Drake and turned him around to face him. 'A Mexican and a real big Indian, you say?'

Drake nodded. 'Yep.'

Bob Lane spat the wooden toothpick from his mouth and rubbed the back of his neck excitedly.

'Zococa!'

'Who?' Drake seemed confused as he watched the eyes of the young lawman dart around.

'Zococa the bandit, Griff.' Lane grinned. 'Only Zococa rides with an Indian. They have a lotta money on their heads.'

'Bandits?'

'Yeah, and they're riding after your stagecoach.' Bob Lane stepped down into the street and headed for the livery stables and his horse.

'What you figuring on doing, Bob?' Drake called out above the sound of music emanating from the saloons.

'Catch me a couple of bandits, Griff,' came the confident reply.

FOUR

The sun was already rising and chasing the shadows into retreat as the galloping six-horse team towed the stagecoach out from the mouth of the mountain pass and began the tricky descent towards the merciless desert. Slowly but surely the perilous trail grew ever wider and sunlight began to lace through the jagged rocks.

Getting to this point had been a miracle in itself as Salty Sagebrush knew by the blood which trickled through his fingers as he held tightly on the huge leather reins. Few drivers even dared to try and control a six-horse team through the twisting trail which led through the sand-coloured mountains in daylight, let alone at night. Yet the crusty old-timer had the eyes of a cat and the courage of a puma.

In this unforgiving land, you needed both in abundance.

Sagebrush had sat on the bouncing high seat and forced the lead horse to increase its speed as they began heading down towards the hot sun-drenched wastes of sand. Josh Willis had clutched his Winchester across his belly for hours as he sat beside the game old cuss who seemed capable of seeing in the dark. His knuckles were white as he held on to the carbine and the edge of the wooden driver's seat as the coach swayed back and forth. Only as the sun raced across the rocks and the land which stretched out into infinity before them, did Willis begin to feel the eyes of the Apaches bearing down on their small vehicle.

For the first time since they had set out from Mission Wells, Josh Willis felt afraid.

It was not the terrifying way in which his partner drove the stagecoach ever onward at breathtaking pace which chilled his bones to their marrow, but the sight which he saw now above them.

A sight that was new to the young stagecoach guard.

There were not dozen or so Apaches up there in the high rocks which overlooked the pass.

There were hundreds.

Willis tapped the shoulder of the old driver and pointed with his thumb to where half-naked warriors seemed to fill every ledge.

'I see 'em,' Sagebrush shouted above the thunderous hoofbeats of his team.

'I don't like it, Salty,' Willis yelled back.

'Me neither,' Sagebrush answered, continuing to concentrate on the twisting trail before his lathered-up horses. There seemed little point in further talk between the pair and they both did their jobs to the best of their abilities, Sagebrush forcing his team to keep up their dangerous pace and Willis clutching his rifle, silently praying he would not be forced to use it.

Choking dust began to fly up over the roof of the stagecoach, coating both driver and guard in a thick layer of yellow grime, yet they continued their daredevil descent. Salty Sagebrush knew this was no time to slow down. For some reason they had a mighty big audience. Each of whom held a bow.

Cracking a long bullwhip above the heads of the galloping team every few minutes, Sagebrush tried to somehow forge his own ceaseless energy into the legs of his six matched horses. It was almost unbearable to be able to see the flat baked plain from their high vantage point without being able to reach it. The trail wove through gigantic boulders but there was no straight route to the flatlands.

It seemed as if they had swallowed a ton of fine dust as Salty Sagebrush dragged the heavy reins hard to his right and watched as the lead horse took the penultimate bend. Now there was a mere half-mile before he could turn the team to his left and drive them out on to the sand. To the passengers inside the stagecoach, it must have been yet another nightmare to add to the many the long journey had inflicted upon them during the night but Sagebrush would not willingly cease his pressure on the team of black horses.

As the stage thundered along the first straight stretch of trail that they had encountered for hours, Josh Willis suddenly noticed that every single Indian had disappeared from above them. He held on to the metal rail which ran all the way around the top of the stagecoach roof, and stared up at the high sand-coloured rock-face.

'Them Apache has gone, Salty.'

Sagebrush nodded.

'That's good, boy. Darn good. I was getting a leetle bit worried back there.'

'Why were they there?' Willis shouted at his partner.

'Who can say. Something must have gotten them riled up,' the old-timer answered.

As he slowed the stagecoach down to make the last turn before they reached the sand-flats, Sagebrush's eyes widened. He had caught sight of something ahead almost hidden in the black shadows of a massive rock.

The old driver hit the brake-pole with his right boot, hauled the hefty reins up to his chest and somehow managed to avoid a pair of men who were standing in the middle of the trail. The stagecoach swayed violently as the six horses drove their hoofs into the soft sand. They stopped within a few feet of the two strange men.

Sagebrush and Willis stared down at the pair, each of whom held on to the horns of his saddle with one hand and his saddle-bags with the other.

Josh Willis raised his Winchester to his shoulder and took careful aim at the pair.

'What you critters doing out here?'

The strange pair moved out into the sun and stared up at the two men on the driver's seat. The older man was rougher and seemed to be in dire need of a shave whilst the other man looked far more dangerous.

'My name's Reno and this is my pal Boyce Lee. We kinda had a run of bad luck back yonder,' the older man replied. He studied the stagecoach long and hard. 'We lost both our horses and want a ride back to someplace civilized.'

'There's a way station about twenty miles away. That's our first stop,' Sagebrush informed the two men.

'That'll do just fine,' Reno grinned.

Salty Sagebrush studied the two men carefully.

He knew they seemed familiar but could not tell where he had seen them before.

'It'll cost ya, boys. The Overland Stage Company ain't no charity.'

'I got me a golden eagle,' Reno said, handing the coin up to the driver. 'Is that enough to buy us a ride?'

Sagebrush's eyes sparkled as he grabbed the coin and pushed it into his shirt-pocket beneath his topcoat.

'I ain't gonna give out no change, Reno.'

'Suits me, old man,' Reno said, casting a quick glance at his companion.

'Toss them saddles up on top and climb in, gents,' Sagebrush beamed toothlessly.

The two men did as instructed. As soon as Sagebrush saw the coach door close, he released the brake and allowed the team to continue.

'Seems a tad odd, Salty,' Willis said as the stage moved out on to the flat sand and began to gather pace.

'You mean about them losing both their horses?'

'Yep.'

'Quit fretting, Josh. We got us a golden eagle to split between us when we reaches the way station.' Sagebrush winked as he slapped the reins across the backs of the team.

'You mean we are gonna keep that gold piece?' Willis gasped innocently.

41

'Sure enough. What the company don't know can't hurt it none.'

Inside the coach, Major Lincoln and Judge Holmes had moved across to sit next to the beautiful Clara King, allowing Reno and Boyce Lee to sit opposite them. As the stage began to rock back and forth once more, nothing was said while both parties studied one another.

'I hope you folks will excuse our appearance,' Reno broke the silence.

'You lost your horses?' Lincoln asked sternly in a manner which bore well for him with soldiers of lesser ranks but grated on most civilians.

'Yep,' Reno replied.

'How?' the major pressed.

'Does it matter?' Lee snapped.

Judge Holmes felt the sweat running down from beneath the band of his hat as he watched the rough-looking pair. Could these men be part of some sort of gang? He began to sweat even more as he started to think about the strong box full of his bank's money reposing beneath Sagebrush.

'You look nervous,' Reno commented to the judge.

'We've had a very rough trip,' Holmes replied. 'We have not been able to sleep.'

'Ain't that a darn shame.' Boyce Lee smiled.

'Hush up. Ain't no call to get mean,' Reno told

42

his partner. He turned his gaze towards Clara King with more than a little interest.

'Remember, gentlemen, there is a lady present,' Major Lincoln said loudly.

'Oh, I sure noticed that, Major,' Reno grinned.

'We ain't blind,' Lee added.

Clara King stared out of the window of the stagecoach at the trail behind them. She had learned long ago that it was always prudent to avoid eye contact with men of this sort.

'I think the major means ...' Holmes tried to speak but was interrupted by Boyce Lee's boot being placed on the seat between the judge's legs.

'We're too old for lectures, old man,' Lee sneered.

Reno rested a hand on his partner's arm and gave him a hard look. Without words, the older man seemed able to make Lee lower his boot back on to the floor.

Just as Reno was about to speak again, to Clara King, he noticed her expression change. Suddenly, she was no longer looking at the passing scenery but at something else. Something which frightened her.

'What's wrong, ma'am?' Reno asked, sliding across the leather seat to the window.

Slowly she raised her gloved hand and pointed fearfully at the dust behind the stage.

Reno leaned his head out of the window and

43

screwed up his eyes until he too saw what was so terrifying.

'What is it, Reno?' Lee asked.

'Apache!'

FIVE

Zococa held the huge stallion in check and pointed a finger down from the golden sun-drenched mountain in the direction of the fleeing stagecoach. At least a hundred Apache warriors were in pursuit of the rocking vehicle as it attempted to find refuge amid the scorching flat landscape. Yet there seemed to be no refuge out there in the white sand.

The Apache lungs were in full war cry as they forced their painted ponies across the desert after the racing six-horse team. The sound of their anger echoed off the mountains as the Mexican bandit stood in his stirrups beside the huge Tahoka.

'This is very bad, I think.'

The eyes of Tahoka narrowed as he watched braves of his own tribe chasing the stagecoach. Even he could not imagine why the six-horse team was being attacked. Yet he knew there had to be a reason, a very good reason.

'It is not any of our business, little rhinoceros,' the bandit said, turning his mount around. Only then did he see the pain etched in the features of his only true friend.

Tahoka raised his right hand and began to point at the cloud of dust rising from the horses' hoofs below them.

'Do you want us to stick our noses into that hornets' nest, *amigo*?' Zococa felt his sweat running cold down his spine as he tried to imagine what fate might await them should they interfere in something they did not understand. 'Even I, the great Zococa, cannot fight with so many of your brothers. Not without reloading my faithful pistol many, many times.'

The giant Apache stared hard at his partner. It was a look which required no words to convey its meaning to the younger man.

Zococa shrugged. 'I think the pretty Clara King would be most grateful if I were to save her from the tomahawks of your fellow Apaches, Tahoka. Maybe we should try and help them. I think Miss King would make love to me if I were victorious.'

The Apache grunted.

Before the Mexican could speak again, the sound of gunfire bounced off the golden boulders around them, startling both their horses. At first

Zococa thought there must be other angry Apaches in the high crags until his keen vision spotted horsemen a quarter-mile above them on the trail. Even at that distance Bob Lane's sheriff's star flashed in the sunlight upon his vest as he led a handful of eager riders craving the reward money upon Zococa's head.

'You are correct little one. We must be brave,' the bandit said. Another bullet flashed past the wide rim of his sombrero as the posse reduced the distance between them.

Tahoka nodded, kicked his heels into the sides of his black mount and rode down on to the flat plain. Without pausing to think, Zococa spurred his pinto into action and raced after the smaller horse. Within a score of paces he had drawn level.

'Ride, Tahoka. Ride,' Zococa screamed across at his friend as their two mounts tore up the dry ground.

The pair of them had no idea what they were doing apart from chasing into the choking dust of the screeching Apaches who were attacking the stagecoach. All the two bandits knew for certain was that five riders were shooting at them and there was nowhere to hide out in the arid wasteland. They had to continue.

To pause, even for a second, meant death. Yet the harder they rode, the closer they got to the hundred or more Indians where death also waited.

Zococa stood in his stirrups, allowing his pinto to keep pace with the slower horse of his friend.

'I do not wish to alarm you, Tahoka, but I think we have just become the meat in the sandwich, *amigo.*'

Suddenly, as the two horses thundered into the choking dust, a volley of shots from the posse behind them caught the attention of the warriors. At least half the braves realized what was happening behind them and swung their mounts around to face the two riders.

Dragging his reins hard to the left, Zococa shouted to his partner to follow him. Tahoka drove his mount after the powerful stallion. Even as their lives hung in the balance, Zococa could not help laughing as he saw the dismayed faces of the posse confronted by so many Indians. Now Sheriff Bob Lane and his followers were no longer chasing and shooting at the two men from south of the border, but trying desperately to stop and turn their own horses before the Apaches overwhelmed them.

'Ride, *amigo,*' Zococa urged his friend as they headed out into the merciless wastes. To their left, they could see the stagecoach still racing for all it was worth, followed by the rest of the braves.

The sound of gunfire was all around them as the bandits sought refuge in a landscape which seemed devoid of sanctuary.

At least nobody seemed to be aiming weapons in their direction any longer, the Mexican thought. Yet as Zococa stared ahead of them there seemed to be nothing but sand as far as the eyes could see.

Only sand.

SIX

It was not the first time that Salty Sagebrush had been required to expertly drive a six-horse team of matched horses beyond their limits to save the hides of his passengers, but it was starting to look as if it might just be the last.

Even a younger man could not have exerted as much power as Sagebrush was capable of as he strained every sinew of his ancient body to maintain the distance between his precious stagecoach and the rampaging Apache riders. It was no easy feat and required skill which only came with years of experience but the old driver had that in abundance. Zigzagging half a dozen horses without overturning the stagecoach was something which was not taught in any books, but should have been. Sagebrush knew that the Apaches would try and kill his horses to bring the vehicle to a halt and the only way of preventing that was to keep them constantly changing direction.

Josh Willis was now lying upon the roof of the rocking vehicle firing his Winchester as the stage sped ever onward. It was not clear if any of his shots were finding their targets as he strained to see through the billowing dust which was being thrown up from the large rear wheels. All the young guard knew for certain was that the luggage around him was filling with deadly arrows as the aim of the chasing warriors became increasingly accurate.

'We ain't got a hope in hell of making it to the way station, Salty,' Josh shouted at the driver.

There was no reply from the toothless Sagebrush. He had more than enough to do just keeping his team of horses on their feet without entering into conversation with anyone. Yet although he did not speak, Sagebrush knew the younger man was right. The team was already noticeably slowing up and there was no way he could get the stagecoach safely to their first port of call. One arrow could cause the entire team to crash into the dry unforgiving ground.

As he cracked the bullwhip above his head for the thousandth time, Sagebrush recalled the old abandoned mission.

'Hang on, Josh boy. I'z got me an idea,' Sagebrush yelled. He wrapped the long heavy reins around his right upper arm and physically dragged the heads of his galloping team until they were aiming east.

'What ya doing?' Willis called out, scrambling across the top of the stagecoach until he was directly behind the old man.

'Just keep shooting, boy,' Sagebrush spat as he forced the vehicle on. 'Try and hit some of them Indians, there's enough of them.'

Apache braves were now nearer than either of them liked and getting closer with every passing second. Josh Willis was cranking the mechanism of his carbine every few seconds and starting to hit what he was aiming at. After he had emptied the first of the rifles he had to clamber down into the driver's box and haul out another before he could continue. Arrows were flying high and wide as their pursuers managed to turn their painted ponies and gallop across their new route.

'Where in tarnation are you heading, Salty?' Josh called out as he saw one of his shots pluck an Apache warrior from his mount.

'Just keep shooting, Josh,' the old-timer replied, slapping the reins down across the backs of his mighty team.

In the distance, through the clouds of dust, Willis could make out the unwelcome sight of the other braves now rejoining the main group.

It was clear that these riders had only one

thought in their minds. They wanted the scalps of the stagecoach's passengers hanging from their war lances.

But why?

Why had things changed?

These Apaches had kept themselves to themselves for years up in their mountain stronghold. They had outwitted even the smartest white man's attempts to locate their camps, by all accounts. What could have brought them down on to the plains and made them attack the stage?

As Josh Willis fired his Winchester at their attackers, he was beginning to doubt his own sanity. He had never knowingly shot another human being in his entire life until this. Now in a matter of less than five minutes he had lost count of how many men his bullets had ripped from the backs of their ponies.

His only consolation was that at least two of their passengers were also firing at the shrieking Apache from the windows of the stage below him. To a man like Josh Willis, it helped to think another man's bullets might be killing their attackers rather than his own.

'You ain't gonna like this, Josh,' Sagebrush shouted.

Willis looked up at the back of his friend. 'I ain't gonna like what, Salty?'

No sooner had the question left the dry lips of

the guard than he knew the answer. Once again the cunning driver hauled the reins of his team sharply to his right and drove straight at the confused Indians, sending them scattering. Only the clouds of dust saved the coach and its occupants from their deadly arrows.

Willis felt the vehicle rocking violently as Sagebrush dragged the heads of his team back to the left and cracked his whip in the air.

Now the stagecoach was racing through its own dust, unseen by the eyes of its enemies.

'You're right. I don't like it,' Josh Willis called out, managing to steady himself on the roof of the stage as half the baggage flew off. 'I can't see them pesky Indians anywhere.'

'And they can't see us, boy,' the older man yelled out, urging the team on and on towards the sight which he knew was their only chance. 'Lookee yonder!'

Josh Willis held on to the back of the driver's seat, then he too saw the sun-baked vision before them. The six horses seemed to sense that there was water within the walls of the old mission and began to find renewed strength.

'What is this place, Salty?'

'Sanctuary, boy,' came the reply.

SEVEN

Salty Sagebrush moved like a man half his age as he leapt from the driver's seat of the stagecoach down on to the dusty ground within the walls of the deserted mission. It had been a long time since he had been forced to stare into the painted face of death, but he still recalled how it was done. It took grit and he still had plenty.

'Git them horses unhitched, Josh,' Sagebrush called out to his younger companion. He raced to the one and only entrance of the high-walled mission, gripping his .45 firmly.

For some reason the Apache warriors did not follow the arrow-riddled vehicle into this place, but remained beyond the high cactus a quarter of a mile away. Maybe it was the tales of the ruthless missionaries who had once dwelt within this sanctuary which kept the Apache at bay. Whatever their reasons were for not following,

Sagebrush was grateful. The old-timer knew there had once been proud wooden gates spanning the archway that he now knelt beside, but they had long ago turned to dust as did everything out in this unforgiving land. With countless hostile Indians just below the massive mountains, he wished the old gates still existed.

Sweat dripped off the ends of his long white shaggy hair as Sagebrush toyed with his pistol and squinted out at the fleeing images of the braves as they gathered on their ponies over the dune beyond the cactus and dead trees. Dust rose into the still air as if mocking the old man as he heard the team of horses being led away from the stage.

The passengers had all disembarked hurriedly within seconds of the stagecoach being brought to a halt but none had ventured anywhere near the old man as he kept silent watch.

'See if there's drinking-water in there, boy,' Sagebrush called out over his scrawny shoulder as he concentrated on the taunting dust out there in the heat haze.

'If there's water anywhere around here, I'll find it,' Willis responded. He approached the shadowy interior of what had obviously once been a stable.

As Josh Willis led the six lathered-up horses into the shade of the building, he felt the hair on the nape of his broad neck rise.

Instinctively, Willis knew he was not alone.

He ran his tongue over his dry, cracked lips as he realized he was not the only human being taking shelter in this cool ancient place.

The sound of a gun-hammer being cocked behind him made Willis drop the heavy reins and turn quickly. His eyes had not managed to adjust to the gloom before he heard another gun-hammer being cocked directly behind him.

Josh Willis raised his arms above his head and desperately tried to focus his eyes. Eyes which were still burning in their sockets from the blazing desert sun and the cruel sand.

'I ain't got no money,' Willis croaked.

The laughter which greeted the dust-caked man came closer until it was right in front of him. Zococa held his silver-plated pistol in his left hand and used his right to rub his jawline.

'I can tell you have no money *señor*. If ever I have seen such a man whose every sinew declared how poverty-stricken he is, it is you.' The bandit smiled as he holstered his gun and stepped close to the stagecoach guard.

Slowly, Willis turned his head and stared into the shadows from where he had heard the first gun-hammer being cocked into position. As the huge Apache came silently forward his heart sank.

'Oh my dear Lord.'

Zococa pointed a finger at the massive Tahoka. 'Put your gun away, my little one. You have frightened our new friend.'

Tahoka slid his pistol into its holster and then moved to the side of the smiling Mexican. He signed with his fingers as he spoke to his companion.

'What's going on?' Willis asked, feeling his heart starting to beat at its normal pace once more. 'Who are you and what the heck is he doing?'

Zococa tilted his head and watched the intricate hand gestures of his friend before replying.

'We are villains, *señor*. Notorious villains. I myself am quite famous and my friend Tahoka speaks with his hands because he has not the tongue any longer.'

'Huh?' Josh Willis felt uneasy as he stared at the stone-featured Apache. 'What ya mean, he ain't got a tongue?'

'Many years ago it was plucked from his mouth by very bad people,' Zococa explained, studying Willis carefully.

'What kinda folks would do such a thing?'

'They did much worse things to my little friend but I, the great Zococa, saved him.' The bandit smiled and stared out into the bright sunshine.

Tahoka began to move his hands once more.

'What's he doing?' Willis asked.

Zococa placed a hand upon the shoulder of the stagecoach guard and whispered into his ear.

'Like I told you, Tahoka's tongue was ripped from his mouth many years ago. He talks to me with his hands.'

'What are you doing here?' Willis asked.

Zococa stepped away from the dusty guard and rested his knuckles on his gunbelt. He smiled broadly.

'Is it not obvious?'

'Not to me it ain't.'

'We have come to rescue you all,' Zococa grinned.

Willis could not quite fathom whether the Mexican was serious. He gathered up the reins of the six-horse team and led them towards the corner of the dark stable and the long water-trough. He placed his hands on the pump and pushed it down, wondering who these strange men were.

'Why are you out here in the middle of this Indian uprising?'

Zococa grinned slowly. He gestured to Tahoka to bring their own mounts to the water-trough.

'We go wherever we want to go.'

'Wait a minute.' Willis suddenly realized to whom he was talking. 'You're Zococa the bandit.'

'*Sí*, the very famous and handsome bandit.'

As water began to trickle from the cast-iron

mouth of the water-pump, Willis cleared his throat.

'You still ain't explained why you boys are out here in the first place, Zococa,' he pressed.

Zococa shrugged. 'The pretty lady named Clara King drove an arrow through my heart and forced me to follow your stagecoach out here. Even a thousand Apache warriors could not stop the heart of Zococa from following.'

'So the strongbox full of money under the driver's seat ain't got nothing to do with you showing up?' Willis asked as the water flowed freely into the trough from the pump.

Zococa grinned.

'*Señor*, you wound me with your tongue.'

EIGHT

The sight of the lean Mexican and the huge
Apache walking a few steps behind Josh Willis
made the stagecoach passengers feel anything but
confident. It was clear to all who watched their
progress toward the kneeling Salty Sagebrush,
that this pair were anything but normal drifters.

'An Indian!' gasped the breathless Clara King,
taking refuge behind the square-shouldered
Major Lincoln.

The officer turned and gave the petite female a
reassuring smile.

'Do not upset yourself, ma'am. I do not think he
is one of the savages who attacked our coach.'

Clara King felt no easier as her eyes followed
the three figures walking towards the archway
where Sagebrush waited and watched.

'I heard tell of a Mexican bandit who rides with
a big Apache, Reno,' Boyce Lee remarked, step-
ping closer to the sweating major.

'Me too,' Reno grunted, checking his pistol. 'Runs by the name of Zococa.'

'Zococa.' Clara King repeated the word without even knowing why she had done so. For some reason the handsome Mexican, who moved like a puma across the sand, interested her. She had never seen anyone quite like him before.

'Do not worry yourself, ma'am,' Major Lincoln said.

Her eyes flashed up at the officer. Without saying anything she had let him know that she was no longer as fearful as she had been.

It took a few moments before Salty Sagebrush sensed that there were three men standing above him in the shadows of the mission entrance. He turned his thin neck and stared beyond the burly Josh, and wondered who this strange twosome were.

'You on our side?'

'*Sí, amigo.*' Zococa smiled as he peered round the wall out into the desert. 'I think we are trapped.'

'You ain't as dumb as you looks, boy.' Sagebrush sniffed and took a long hard look at the massive Tahoka. 'Is that Indian safe to have around?'

Tahoka's eyes flashed angrily at the old man, then he looked at his companion.

Zococa placed a hand upon the heaving chest of the warrior.

'Tahoka is easily upset, my friend. Please do not hurt his feelings because he is a man whom it is wise to have on your side in a situation such as this.'

Sagebrush got to his feet and nodded at the two men.

'I'm just a tad worried. This ain't the sort of place you can defend easily.'

'Why do we not push the stage into the gap, old one?' Zococa suggested.

Sagebrush raised his white eyebrows and nodded.

'That's a damn good idea, young 'un.'

Zococa walked to the stagecoach behind the driver and guard and watched as the passengers reluctantly began to approach. All except the beautiful Miss King.

Moving the body of the vehicle into the archway was simple with so many willing and able hands.

'At least them redskins can't ride in here now,' Judge Holmes said, standing beside the wooden coach. The other men gathered around Zococa and his massive partner.

'It will slow them up but not stop them altogether, *señor*,' Zococa commented. He found a long cigar in his jacket-pocket and placed it between his perfect teeth. 'Only God himself can stop an Apache if he's determined enough.'

'Get the strongbox down from under the driver's

seat Sagebrush,' Judge Holmes demanded.

Reno ran his fingers down his unshaven face as he heard the words. He looked into Boyce Lee's eyes. Nothing was said between the pair. Nothing had to be said.

As Josh Willis climbed up on to the stage to get the bullion-box, the old driver rested a hand on the judge's shoulder and sighed heavily.

'For a judge, you ain't too smart.'

'I beg your pardon?' Holmes looked outraged.

Sagebrush smoothed his beard down with the fingers of his free hand and continued. 'I figure there are about two more folks here now who know about your money. Folks who might not have had any idea you was transporting a lot of money. Just because you opened your mouth.'

'Is there much money in the strongbox, *señor*?' Zococa smiled as he moved beside the banker and stared out at the rising dust beyond the dunes.

Judge Holmes felt his face burning as blood rushed to his cheeks.

'Why do you ask?'

'I am a bandit. It is my duty to ask.'

Holmes watched the smiling profile. 'For a minute there I thought you were serious.'

Zococa raised an eyebrow and turned his head until he was facing the man. 'I think you will be the richest man in heaven if those Apaches attack.'

Judge Holmes felt his heart beginning to pound beneath his fine clothes.

NINE

By the time the ferocious sun had reached directly overhead, the occupants of the old mission knew they were trapped with no possible way of escaping the Apache braves mustered beyond the sand dunes below their mountain stronghold.

The same question filled all their minds: what had caused the normally peaceful Apache to suddenly attack their stagecoach with such fury? What had happened to change things so drastically? If there were answers, they were not forthcoming to the group of trapped people huddled inside the adobe walls.

All that was certain was they had a fight on their hands. A bloody fight which would cost lives. Perhaps all their lives.

For men such as Salty Sagebrush this was just another moment when they had to face the unknown dangers this perilous land had a habit of throwing at them. He had been in hundreds of such scrapes over his unnumbered decades of weary existence, but none quite as daunting as this.

For Major Lincoln this was an annoying reminder that however close he was to retirement, he had not reached his pension just yet.

The strange duo of Boyce Lee and his partner Reno knew they had managed to escape the merciless desert by hitching a ride upon the stagecoach but now they too were trapped within the confines of the ancient edifice, like all the others. Had they eluded death or simply delayed its inevitable arrival?

Josh Willis knew nothing of the wars waged in these lands or of the men who waged them. All his thoughts could concentrate upon was the face of his beautiful wife waiting back in Mission Wells for his safe return. A return that, he knew, might never happen if things continued to disintegrate in this hopeless place.

Judge Holmes had little on his mind except the strongbox he had brought from his bank and which he now sat upon in the cool shade of the only habitable room within the walls of the mission. For him the danger outside was little more than an irritation which was stopping him from getting to where he wanted to go. Why he was transporting so much money out of Mission Wells was known only to him. Holmes was not about to explain his actions to anyone.

Clara King had walked back and forth more than a hundred times within the cool room which faced the archway now blocked by the stagecoach. She seemed unable to sit down on any of the wooden benches that faced the high north wall upon which the outline of a huge cross could still be clearly seen. Her eyes fixed on the men who moved around the coach as if trying to come up with some grand plan that would save their bacon. Whatever Clara King was thinking, nobody could tell what it was by the expression which masked her face. For her, this was a nightmare.

It seemed that only the tall, rangy Mexican who so casually leaned against the stagecoach and puffed on his long cigars made any real impression on her. Even in the darkness of the long cool room, she could feel his eyes seeking and finding her as she passed the doorway.

Could he see her? He claimed to be a bandit but she wondered if anyone who smiled so freely could actually belong to that profession.

As the giant Tahoka climbed up the side of the wall and rested on top of the archway, Clara King wondered who these men really were. The Indian looked so frightening, yet he appeared to do everything the young Zococa ordered.

Without question, this was the strangest group of people to find themselves thrown together. Perhaps only the beautiful female was capable of judging any of them with any accuracy but even she could not see within their souls.

For even the wisest of people cannot see how black another's heart might truly be under the cover of their fine garments.

'I request a horse, sir,' Major Lincoln boomed down into Sagebrush's ear as the stagecoach driver eyed up the dust beyond the dune of sand.

'What in tarnation iz you squawking about, Major?' the old-timer asked, beating the dust off his hat against the side of the stagecoach.

'I have decided to take command of the situation,' Lincoln informed him.

'Well that's a darn generous thing for you to do.' Sagebrush glanced around the faces of Zococa, Reno and Lee as he spoke.

'Get one of the horses and I shall ride for help.' The major stared through the open windows of the vehicle at the distant dune where dust still rose. 'I am a cavalry officer and the person most suited to this sort of thing. I can get help back here within a few hours.'

Sagebrush looked at the wide girth of the man.

'You looks like you ain't had much practice riding anything harder than a desk lately, Major.'

Lincoln's face grew redder. 'I order you to get

me a horse. The pinto stallion will do.'

Zococa stared from beneath the brim of his wide sombrero at the officer and cleared his throat.

'I do not think I can let you take my horse, *señor*.'

'Are you defying a United States Cavalry officer, sir?' The major marched up to the Mexican and glared into his eyes.

'*Sí señor*. I am most sorry but I must refuse your gracious offer to take my most beautiful stallion out into the desert so those Indians can kill it.'

'I am doing this for the sake of the other passengers,' Major Lincoln stated.

Zococa walked away from the coach, then glanced back at the soldier.

'I think you are doing it just to get another medal.'

Lincoln's face went even redder.

'I protest, sir.'

'You have enough medals, Major.' Zococa grinned and drew his silver pistol swiftly from its holster, allowing the cavalry officer to see how fast he was with the weapon. 'I am unwilling for you to take my horse to certain death.'

Lincoln turned back towards the other men.

'It's suicidal, Major,' Lee said, strolling up to the army man. 'I figure our best bet is to sit it out. There's plenty of water here. Them Apaches might get bored and head on home in a few hours.'

'There might be enough water but ...' Lincoln began.

'But no grub,' Sagebrush muttered, scratching his white beard. 'We iz a tad shy on grub, boys.'

Major Lincoln rested a hand on the skinny shoulder of the old-timer.

'I implore you to let me use one of the coach-horses. I happen to know that there are at least thirty cavalrymen not more than ten miles from this very spot, Sagebrush.'

Sagebrush blinked hard.

'Soldiers? Out here? How come?'

'Building a bridge over the Red River at Hooper's Point,' came the reply.

Reno grabbed at Boyce Lee's sleeve when he had digested the major's words. There was a look of concern in his face which only Zococa seemed to see as he walked slowly around the group.

'I think you will have a hard time getting away from the Indians, *señor*.' Zococa frowned and he pushed his sombrero up off his forehead with the barrel of his gun. 'Apache ponies are very fast. Much faster than any of our mounts.'

'I learned to ride at West Point, sir,' Lincoln announced.

Zococa shrugged. He watched the beautiful female moving gracefully across the courtyard towards them.

'Did I hear you say there are soldiers nearby, Major?'

The bandit liked her voice. It matched her looks. Soft and sweet.

'The major thinks there are soldiers nearby, pretty lady.'

Clara King dismissed the words of the bandit as she stood between Sagebrush and Lincoln.

'Are you sure there are troopers out there, Major?'

'I drew up the orders personally, ma'am,' Lincoln said. 'I know exactly where they are and the swiftest way of reaching them.'

'But it's dang dangerous,' Sagebrush said with a sigh. 'Even for a young 'un, it'd be a mighty risky ride.'

'Not as dangerous as starving to death, man.' Lincoln glared down at the bearded face. For the first time since the officer had started talking, his true concern showed in every weathered line of his face. He was not asking, he was pleading.

Sagebrush looked around at the faces of the others. Then he nodded.

'Go get one of the stagecoach horses, Major. Compliments of the Overland Stage Company.'

'I'll need a saddle.' Lincoln's voice was now lower.

Zococa waved for Tahoka to come down from his high vantage point. As the enormous Indian reached his side, the Mexican spoke:

'Let the major have your saddle, Tahoka.'

Tahoka gestured with his hands.

'I will buy you a new one when we have funds, little one,' Zococa said, glancing in the direction of Judge Holmes who was standing in the doorway of the building. 'I think we will not have to go far to find the money.'

Tahoka nodded.

As Major Lincoln followed the tall Indian towards the stables, Clara King turned and looked into the handsome face of Zococa, who was biting his lower lip.

'You have suddenly stopped smiling, Zococa. Why?'

Zococa shook his head.

'I think the major will get killed and if he does I will have to buy Tahoka a new saddle.'

'But if the major is successful, we will be rescued,' Clara King added.

Without saying another word, the bandit followed the two men into the stable.

'What on earth is wrong with Zococa, Mr Sagebrush?' Clara King asked the old man who was shaking his ancient head as if he, too, were troubled.

'Zococa and his Indian friend are wanted on both sides of the border, ma'am. Dead or alive,' Salty Sagebrush replied.

'You mean that if the major is successful and

73

does manage to bring the troopers back here, they will arrest them both?' Her voice shook as the words left her red lips.

'Nope. I doubt if they'll arrest them. They'll lynch the poor bastards for sure.' Sagebrush turned and headed back to Josh Willis.

Five minutes later Major Lincoln rode a large brown horse from the stables toward the mission archway. The strong arms of Josh Willis pushed the coach a few feet away from the wall as the cavalry officer approached.

'Good luck, Major,' Sagebrush said.

Lincoln saluted and rode the mount through the narrow gap out into the baking desert. As Willis and Salty pushed the vehicle back into place, they could hear the spine-chilling sounds of Apache warriors chasing the major.

Nothing was said as the sound grew fainter.

Clara King felt her heart racing as she walked back to the cool building once more. She wanted the major to be successful and bring help but feared what might happen to the tall handsome bandit and his faithful comrade.

She had never seen a man hanged before and did not want to start now.

TEN

The two weather-beaten riders who came thundering down from the high mesa had barely enough time to rein in their mounts before the first wave of arrows came flying in from the Apache warriors ranged between them and the crumbling mission.

Tate Morse and his partner Charlie Higgs had been scouts for the army and stagecoach companies for the better part of a decade and had seen more Indians than most souls, but nothing like the sight which faced them on this hot blistering afternoon.

They alone had managed to travel through the forbidden land of the Apache unscathed. Until now.

Now they were targets.

Morse, being the older and wiser of the pair, was first to spot the paint on the sun-burned faces of the braves as they felt the arrows passing over their heads.

'What in tarnation…?'

Charlie Higgs dragged his reins around and tried to work out what they had ridden into.

'We gotta get us some distance from them bucks, Tate.'

Morse felt his mouth drying as he caught sight of the half-dozen Apache braves who had thrown themselves on to the backs of their ponies and started up the rise towards them, leaving the main group of warriors sheltering below the massive sand dune.

Both frantic scouts turned their horses in the direction of the mountains and dug their spurs deeply into the lathered-up flesh. The creatures began to climb the dry dusty rock-face slowly as the sound of their pursuers drew closer and closer.

Morse had hardly managed to get his mount balanced before he felt the heat of an arrowhead tearing through the thick leather chaps which covered his legs. As his eyes darted to his leg he could see the blood-soaked shaft of the arrow protruding through his flesh.

Blood squirted out from both entry and exit points of the wound.

The scream which the older man let out caused Higgs to drag his horse around to see what had befallen his friend.

'Tate! Tate!'

Morse pulled his trusty long rifle from its resting place beneath the saddle and cranked the mechanism as he felt blood filling his right boot.

'We ain't gonna get these horses back up there, Charlie.'

Higgs knew his partner was right and he too pulled out his carbine, holding his mount in check with his legs. Without another word passing between the two men they both began firing at the screaming Indians.

It took at least two dozen shots to fell all of the galloping braves who had broken free of the main war-party.

Holding their smoking rifles in one hand and their reins in the other the two men rode quickly across the flat ridge as they heard more Apaches closing in on them.

Another four or five had leapt on the backs of their ponies and started up the steep rock-face after the fleeing scouts. The air seemed filled with their shrieks.

The Indian ponies were smaller and more used to the loose rocky surface. With each heartbeat they got closer to the pair of bemused riders who were trying vainly to find a place of safety amid the blistering hot boulders.

There seemed no escape from them. Arrows flew overhead as the expert Indian riders somehow managed to guide their mounts whilst at the same time using their deadly bows.

Crashing through a wall of dead brushwood, both men allowed their horses to leap down into a dark gully before steadying the frightened creatures.

It was the bleeding Tate Morse who first saw the narrow gap below the rocks and steered his horse down into its dark shadowy depths. Higgs galloped after his friend, trying to keep low in his saddle as he saw the glistening arrowheads flying from the small lethal bows. The two men had barely reached the middle of the narrow pathway when they heard the hoofbeats of the ponies behind them echoing off the rocky heights.

'Ride fast, Tate,' Higgs implored the older man as he trailed him along the narrow route.

Morse sank his spurs into his horse again and forced the animal to gallop faster than it had ever done before. Yet no matter how fast the older scout went it did not help Higgs. There was barely enough width for one horse to negotiate the twisting narrow trail and Charlie Higgs was following his wounded comrade, unable to draw level or pass even though his horse was the faster of the two. Behind him the Indians were closing the gap with every stride of their ponies and soon the leader of the pack would use his bow.

'How much further?' Higgs called out, trying to

cock his carbine with one hand as he galloped behind the tail of Morse.

There was no answer.

Tate Morse was driving his mount with every ounce of his draining strength as he felt the agony of the arrow in his right leg tearing through his body. The narrow route seemed to the older scout to be going downhill, but he could not see anything but walls of rock before his burning eyes.

They had to reach the desert floor soon, Morse thought. It had to be close. It just had to be.

Twisting one way then another, Morse guided the steaming horse on and on.

Now he was desperate. Now he felt his life flowing from his tired body with every drop of blood which squirted from the wound. This was not a place to die, he thought, as he dragged the reins to his right and aimed the horse down another steep incline.

Somewhere along this strange trail there had to be a way out on to the sandy plain and hopefully a clear run to the old mission.

He had to keep going for both their sakes. To allow himself to pass out here would mean certain death, not just for himself but for his partner.

Morse allowed his rifle to slip from his grip as he tried to get a better grip on the leather reins.

Then he heard the sound of Charlie Higgs's

rifle firing at their followers behind him. The sound was deafening as it bounced off the solid rocks all around them. The single shot echoed for ever in Morse's tired head as he forced the animal beneath him to even greater speed.

There was no time to look back to see what result the bullet might have had. No time for anything but holding on to the reins of the crazed mount as it raced on and on in blind obedience to its master's commands.

Suddenly, a shaft of light faced the weeping eyes of the leading rider as he rode round a bend. Bright blinding sunlight told Tate Morse that he had finally reached the elusive plain.

The desert was stretched out before him like a golden vision of hope. Yet before the older scout had ridden twenty yards across the hot sand he heard a spine-chilling scream behind him.

Stopping his sweat-drenched horse, Tate Morse turned just in time to see Higgs being thrown headlong over the neck of his stricken mount as an arrow found the creature's heart. Morse watched in horror as he saw his friend bouncing across the dry parched ground towards him. It was a limp, lifeless sort of bounce. Morse wondered if Charlie was dead or just knocked cold.

Pulling his pistol from his deep jacket-pocked, Morse rode back towards his friend as the first of the Apache braves appeared out of the narrow rocky gully.

Morse had never been the best of shots but seeing that the warrior was blinded by the blazing sun he fired and watched as the Apache fell from his pony.

Riding closer to where Higgs lay, Morse cocked his gun again and waited for the next Indian to appear. It was only a few seconds but it seemed an eternity to the wounded scout. This time it took two shots to despatch his target.

Once again, the old scout felt no satisfaction from his accuracy, only confusion. What had turned these peaceful Apaches on to the warpath?

Hovering over the motionless Charlie Higgs, Morse waited again and this time managed to kill the Apache as soon as the rider rode out of the dark trail and into the bright sunlight.

'You still alive, Charlie?' Morse yelled at his friend when the last of the braves rode out on to the sandy plain. Holding his pistol at arm's length, Morse squeezed the trigger and heard the hammer falling on to an empty chamber. For a brief terrifying moment, he wondered if his pistol was out of ammunition.

His blood ran cold as he clawed at the hammer again with his thumb. The Apache was riding straight at him with his bow raised as Morse managed to pull the trigger again.

This time there was an explosive blast which filled the air with black gunpowder.

There was a haunting sound from the throat of the Indian as the bullet hit him squarely in the chest. It was the sound of death. The pony raced across the sand as its master rolled lifelessly off its back.

'Charlie!' Morse shouted again.

Somehow the younger scout had survived his fall and began to crawl towards Morse's stirrup.

'My horse,' Higgs said, as he clambered to his feet beside the blood-soaked leg of the older scout.

'It's a goner, Charlie. Haul yourself up on the back of my horse fast,' Morse urged. He dropped his gun back into his jacket-pocket and tried to get his eyes to focus.

Higgs held on to the saddle, stepped into the loose stirrup and pulled himself up behind his partner.

'You on?' Morse growled as pain once more ripped through his leg.

'Yep.'

Morse dragged his reins hard around and urged his mount on with a kick of his left spur. The animal somehow managed to gallop on towards the mission buildings.

Then they saw them.

Nearly a hundred of them to their left, sitting astride their painted ponies.

Now they had to try and run the gauntlet.

It was only a thousand feet to the ancient build-ing, but every single one of those feet held the possibility of death.

ELEVEN

Zococa was first to race to the stagecoach, jammed in the archway of the mission, with his silver-plated pistol gripped firmly in his left hand.

'Quickly, old one. Help me move the stagecoach.'

'What is it, boy?' Sagebrush asked when he crawled from beneath the body of the wooden vehicle to stand beside the bandit.

'I think the Indians have found another target,' Zococa said resting his back against the wall and squinting out into the dazzling sunlight at the horse racing towards them. He began pushing the heavy weight.

Sagebrush grabbed the large rear wheel and turned it until the coach started to move away from the adobe wall.

'How did ya know them guys were coming, Zococa?' he asked as he saw the horse thundering towards the mission with the two scouts on its back.

'Tahoka told me with his hands, *amigo*.' The bandit sighed and rubbed the sweat from his face on to his jacket sleeve.

The Apache braves were now making enough noise to wake the dead as they fired their lethal arrows at the pitiful horse which was trying desperately to get to the crumbling mission.

When only a matter of a dozen yards from the safety of the high walls, the beast fell, its body riddled with arrows.

'Oh my dear Lord!' Sagebrush exclaimed.

Without a second's hesitation Zococa moved quickly away from the wall and gave the pair of crawling men cover with his pistol until they reached the arms of Sagebrush.

'You're out of ammo. Git back in here, boy,' the stagecoach driver screamed at the bandit as he dragged two stunned scouts into the mission courtyard.

Coolly emptying the spent shells from his gun, Zococa walked backwards as arrows fell all about him.

'Do not fret, old man. They have not got the range to hit the great Zococa.' The bandit smiled and started sliding bullets into the empty chambers of the Colt.

As the other men pushed the stagecoach back

into the archway, Sagebrush accepted a canteen of water from Josh Willis. Then he knelt down beside the two exhausted scouts.

'Iz you brave or just a leetle bit loco, Zococa?' he asked the tall bandit.

Zococa smiled and dropped the silver pistol back into its holster.

'I am crazy.'

'That was bravery, young man,' said Judge Holmes, patting the shoulder of the bandit. He knelt down beside the two scouts and Sagebrush.

Tahoka climbed down from the wall and stood beside his partner, gesturing with his hands.

Leaning close to the huge Indian, Zococa whispered:

'I agree, my little rhinoceros. It will be very hard to rob someone who is so flattering. Hard but not impossible.'

Sagebrush handed the canteen of water to the pair of exhausted scouts. Then he looked up at the handsome Mexican.

'You could have been torn apart by them redskins' arrows.'

'This is very true.' Zococa smiled. 'Maybe the good judge is correct when he says I am brave.'

'What courage!' Judge Holmes reiterated.

Boyce Lee and Reno had been watching everything without moving a muscle to help. They had moved away from the other men soon after Major

Lincoln had ridden out on his quest for help. Yet it seemed that Willis and Sagebrush had not noticed the distance the pair had suddenly put between them. Nor had the wealthy banker. Clara King was grateful that the two dishevelled strangers no longer seemed interested in her. She saw no point in questioning their motives. She had other more important things on her mind.

Things which haunted her.

Only Zococa and his trusty Indian friend seemed to be aware of the pair's strange behaviour.

'What happened to you boys?' Sagebrush asked Tate Morse while he inspected the blood-soaked arrow protruding through the man's leg.

'Everything has gone damned crazy,' More responded, buckling to the pain which continued to tear through his bruised and battered body.

'Them Apache ain't never been hostile,' Charlie Higgs added. He took another long swallow from the canteen. 'Me and Tate have been riding this land for ten summers or more and they've always been peaceful.'

'What could have caused them to go on the war path?' Zococa asked.

Higgs looked up at the Mexican.

'I was hoping you boys had some answers.'

Zococa stared across at Reno and Lee. Then he turned to Tahoka.

'It might be wise if you were to climb the high wall over the stable, *pequeño.*'

Tahoka nodded and strode across the courtyard, carrying his rifle across his chest.

'Help me get this man into the building, Josh,' Sagebrush said anxiously. 'I gotta try and get this arrow out of his leg before he bleeds to death.'

'How come you sent your big friend over there, Zococa?' Josh Willis asked as he helped Sagebrush lift Tate Morse off the ground.

'I do not wish for Tahoka's horse or my magnificent stallion to be stolen, *amigo,*' the bandit replied as Judge Holmes helped Charlie Higgs to his feet.

'You figure Reno and Lee might try and steal your horses?'

'*Sí.* There is something I do not trust about those two men.'

As the two stagecoach men helped the injured Morse towards the building Zococa walked beside them, staring in the direction of the watching Lee and Reno.

Morse was carried into the cool interior of the mission, and Zococa paused as Judge Holmes walked in behind the men. From beneath the wide black brim of his sombrero he tried to work out what the two churlish men were planning.

It took a thief to recognize a thief.

Zococa knew that these men were no drifting

cowboys, or anything else honourable for that matter. Yet they were also totally unlike himself. Reno and Lee were made of a different cloth.

Their sort was harder to figure.

Pushing his sombrero up off his temple with his long index finger, Zococa glanced up to the roof of the stable where Tahoka sat, clutching his Winchester across his waist.

The Apache brave nodded.

Zococa made his way slowly towards the pair of well-armed men.

TWELVE

The three men stared at each other for what seemed an eternity in mutual awe. Reno was the more physical of the two strangers yet even he was cautious and deliberate in his actions in case the mysterious Zococa took any quick hand movement as a threat. The bandit, in turn, knew these men were unlike all the other men with whom he found himself trapped inside the mission. These were killers. He recognized the tell-tale signs that characterized all men who lived by their prowess with their weaponry. There was a look in the eyes of cold-blooded killers which he had seen so many times during his life.

It was as if nature itself had branded their tanned brows with a warning sign. Zococa was unafraid but duly cautious.

'What you looking at, Zococa?' Reno asked

angrily as the bandit paused a mere yard from the pair. They were resting beside a dried pile of rubble which had once been a wall.

'You ought to keep your distance, boy,' Boyce Lee added, aiming a dirty finger at the face of Zococa. 'It ain't wise for a nosy Mex to get too interested in Americans.'

'It is not wise to get too ambitious, *señor*,' Zococa said, watching as the men rose from the wall to their full height.

'You don't scare me, Zococa,' Reno snarled. Boyce Lee stood shoulder to shoulder with him.

Zococa's eyes glanced down at the saddle-bag between the feet of the older man. He had noticed that neither man allowed this particular bag out of their sight, while they had left the other on top of the stagecoach unattended.

What was in the saddle-bag? Zococa wondered. It was a question the bandit knew might not be easy to answer.

'You better play safe and leave us alone, Zococa,' Lee uttered in a tone which would have scared most men but did not impress the bandit.

'There is something about you boys which makes me concerned, *amigos*,' Zococa said. He allowed his left hand to hover above the grip of his pistol.

'If you know what's good for you I figure you ought to keep clear of me and Reno,' Lee warned the smiling bandit. 'Any man wanted dead or alive like you ought to steer clear of seasoned gunfighters.'

'Gunfighters?' Zococa smiled even more widely. 'I had thought perhaps you were in the same line of work as my humble self.'

'You thought we was outlaws like you?' Reno laughed and took a step closer to the Mexican. 'I ought to kill you now to save time when the cavalry get here.'

'I would try not to be so brave, *amigo*. Many men have made the simple mistake of underestimating Zococa,' the bandit dryly advised.

'You ain't gonna live long enough for them soldiers to do a lynchin', boy,' Lee drawled coldly.

'If the Indians attack, I think none of us will live to see the sunset, my friend.' Zococa raised an eyebrow, suspecting that the pair of men before him had as much to fear from the cavalry as he had.

'Yeah?' Reno tilted his head and flexed his fingers above his holstered gun.

'At least we don't ride with one of the savages, like you,' Lee added meanly.

Zococa's eyes glanced up at the stable roof just long enough for Boyce Lee to follow his gaze. Seeing Tahoka aiming the Winchester in their direction made the older man touch the shoulder of his partner.

'Reno!'

'What?' Reno snapped.

'That giant Apache has a bead on us, Reno,' Lee warned.

Zococa smiled and touched the brim of his hat. He walked away from the pair, back towards the archway and the lone figure of Charlie Higgs who was still staring out at the Indians beyond the dune.

'Them critters friends of yours?' Higgs asked as Zococa reached his side and stared through the windows of the stagecoach.

'I think not, *amigo*,' Zococa said. He tried not to allow the guns behind him to take his mind from the taunting warriors out there in the afternoon sun.

'I still can't figure out what could have got them Apaches all riled up,' Higgs said, and sighed as he nursed his skinned face with one of his bruised hands.

Zococa glanced over his shoulder at the two men standing in the centre of the courtyard. He wondered whether they had the answer, or perhaps it lay hidden in the saddle-bag at their feet.

THIRTEEN

The smoke which trailed upward into the cloudless blue sky gave no hint of the reasons behind the Apache fury. As Zococa lay against the crumbling adobe bricks above the missing archway, he could only wonder. The sun was now lower in the sky yet still hot enough to burn the skin off any unsuspecting creature stupid enough to dwell too long in its merciless rays. Soon it would set but would darkness offer them more protection or just multiply the dangers?

As Salty Sagebrush climbed up to the well sheltered vantage-point, the bandit said nothing.

'War smoke!' Sagebrush exclaimed, resting on his belly beside the silent Mexican.

'Sí, amigo. I think the Indians are now getting serious.'

Sagebrush gave a long heavy sigh as his old

eyes tried to count the fleeting images of Apache braves beyond the long high dune of sand.

'Did you save the life of the injured scout, *amigo?*' Zococa broke the silence between them.

'It was a leetle bit tricky but I think I managed to stop the bleeding,' Sagebrush responded.

'Will he be of any help to us in our present predicament?'

'Hell no. He'll probably sleep until morning.'

Zococa shook his head. This was not getting any better, he thought. In fact it seemed to be getting worse with every passing heartbeat.

With a whistle from his toothless mouth, Sagebrush managed to get Josh Willis to scramble up from the mission courtyard.

'What ya want, Salty?' Willis asked, staring out with innocent eyes at the smoke rising up into the heavens.

'Find all the Winchesters and ammunition in the stagecoach box and dish it out to the other men, Josh,' Sagebrush ordered, trying to maintain his composure.

Before Willis could respond to the old driver's words, Zococa gripped his arm.

'I would not give a weapon to our quiet friends.'

'You mean Reno and Lee?' Willis asked staring hard into the bandit's face.

'*Sí*. They have enough weapons of their own,' Zococa nodded.

Josh Willis turned and looked at Sagebrush as if seeking confirmation of the last instructions.

'Reckon Zococa is right, boy. Best not tempt fate,' Sagebrush said.

Both men watched as the muscular Willis climbed down from the high wall.

'You figure them two varmints might be dangerous?'

Zococa nodded and turned to look at the smoke drifting up into the sky before them.

'Them two have been worrying me since we picked them up out there on the trail,' Sagebrush spat. 'It don't figure on two riders losing their mounts at the same time.'

'Maybe they know why the Apaches are so angry, *amigo*,' Zococa said, trying vainly to think of a way out of this perilous situation. No matter how hard he concentrated, there seemed to be no easy answers.

'Reckon you could be right.' Sagebrush ran his fingers through his long white mane of hair as he also tried to think of a solution to their plight.

For several minutes both men did nothing but look at the smoke which continued to rise from beyond the sand dunes like a warning of what was yet to come.

'You read Indian smoke, boy?'

Zococa shook his head, then thought of Tahoka across the courtyard, perched upon the stable rooftop.

'I do not, but my little comrade can.'

Sagebrush watched as the Mexican turned and began to make hand-signals to his friend. Without a second's hesitation, the huge Apache brave rose and began to walk towards them across the ruins of the once proud wall.

'I can't figure why them Indians ain't just attacked,' Salty Sagebrush mumbled under his breath.

Zococa glanced at the troubled man beside him.

'Maybe they do not want us but someone within our midst?'

Sagebrush nodded in agreement.

'That sounds right. I heard tell that you done killed more than a hundred men.'

Zococa grinned.

'I too have heard these stories about myself.'

'Ain't it true?'

'A slight exaggeration, *señor*.'

Neither man spoke again until Tahoka was at their side kneeling on the crumbling top of the wall.

'Can you read the smoke, my little one?' Zococa asked his friend.

Tahoka nodded and looked long and hard at the plumes of smoke which rose up from the distant stronghold of the Apache. As he watched the smoke his hands translated the meaning to his younger friend.

'What he say, boy?' Sagebrush asked as he watched the Indian, whose expressionless face stared out into the shimmering heat haze.

'He says they mean to attack at first light in the morning,' Zococa replied quietly.

'I figure there has to be more than a hundred of them Indians out there,' Sagebrush said, sighing heavily. 'If they attack, we ain't got a chance.'

Tahoka began to gesture once more with his hands to the worried bandit. This time there seemed more urgency in his hand movements. This time he was telling the young bandit something which he knew the Mexican did not wish to hear. Tahoka was telling Zococa what he intended to do and that there was no point in arguing.

When Tahoka made up his mind about something, there was no living creature who stood a chance of making him change it.

'What's he saying now, Zococa?' Sagebrush asked as he saw the expression of the handsome bandit alter.

Zococa lost his smile as he settled himself on to his belly once more.

'Tahoka says he will slip through the gateway after dark and make his way into the heart of the Apache encampment.' Zococa felt his throat tighten as the words began to choke him.

'But that's plumb loco, boy,' Sagebrush gasped.

'They'll kill him for sure even if he is one of their tribe.'

Zococa swallowed hard but no words managed to escape his troubled mouth. He knew the old man was probably right.

FOURTEEN

Tahoka stripped off his shirt as the sun finally sank out of sight and the desert was enveloped in darkness. For only a few moments did the three men see the horrific scars upon the upper torso of the huge Apache's chest and back. For Sagebrush and Josh Willis the sight had been something they had not expected. No man could have survived such torture, yet the silent Tahoka had done so.

For Zococa, the sight of his friend's scars were mere reminders of the day long ago when he had saved the warrior. Only Zococa knew the true magnitude and scale of the injuries his mute friend had suffered at the hands of the unknown vermin who walked on two legs like real human beings. The bandit remembered how he had found Tahoka with his tongue torn from his mouth. A thousand knife cuts had practically removed the flesh from the giant and yet he had somehow clung to life. Zococa recalled how they had taken not just his tongue but his manhood.

The massive Indian stood beside the stage-coach, waiting for darkness to shield him from the eyes of his fellow Apaches.

'This is madness, my little one,' Zococa said to the Indian who stood clutching his knife in his right hand, waiting for the exact time when he knew he could move across the sand without being observed.

Tahoka looked down at the bandit and nodded.

It was not the nod of a man agreeing with another's statement but the nod of someone acknowledging a debt he knew would always be impossible to repay.

'You will go out there, whatever I say?' Zococa asked.

Tahoka rested a huge hand upon the arm of the Mexican and grunted softly. Before Zococa had stopped shaking his head he realized something.

The giant Indian was gone.

Zococa dropped on to one knee, screwed up his eyes and stared out into the prairie, trying desperately to see where his friend had gone. Soon Charlie Higgs, Sagebrush and Josh Willis had joined him in the dust, watching the black-ness for a glimpse of the huge Indian. Tahoka had not lost any of his natural cunning though, and had disappeared.

'He's an Indian, Zococa,' said Sagebrush into his ear. 'He's an Apache. If anyone can get close to them, it's him.'

Zococa shook his head again.

'He might be an Apache but he is also my friend, *amigo*. My only friend.'

Higgs rested a hand on the broad shoulder of the Mexican.

'Stop fretting. I done seen a lot of Indians in my time as a scout but none like him. The first thing I noticed about him was that even though he's big, his feet don't make no sound when he walks.'

'Charlie's right, son,' Sagebrush agreed.

Zococa nodded. 'This is true, but if they capture him, how will I know? Even if they torture him, Tahoka cannot scream out like other men. Tahoka cannot let me know.'

The massive body of the Apache slid across the sand towards the dunes, unseen and unheard. Tahoka had indeed not lost any of his natural cunning as a hunter and knew exactly how to get within a few feet of his chosen prey without being spotted.

Yet Tahoka did not want to kill any of the braves who laid siege to the old mission. He wanted to try to find out why they had suddenly chosen to make war after so many years of living peacefully.

Tahoka dragged himself over the edge of the dune and allowed himself to slide silently down into the gully below, where he lay outstretched. Only his eyes moved as he surveyed the scene about him. To his right, a line of ponies ate the grain their masters had scattered over the ground.

Directly ahead, the braves huddled around dozens of small fires, eating and talking.

Tahoka remained motionless as his eyes sought out and located the sentry he knew would be guarding the precious mounts. Rolling over several times, Tahoka's body came to a halt beside a boulder.

Instinctively the huge warrior knew how to remain downwind of both men and animals as he crawled on all fours around the herd of tethered ponies towards the Apache guard.

Closer and closer he got to the Indian who stood wrapped in a blanket at the very edge of the tethered horses. Then, faster than the blink of an eye, Tahoka struck.

Rising up from the sand, Tahoka managed to grab the face of the sentry with one hand, muffling his mouth with his large palm whilst striking the back of the Apache's skull with the clenched fist of his other hand.

The sentry staggered, pulled his razor-sharp knife from his belt and lunged forward. Tahoka held on to the mouth of the Apache as tightly as he could as the blade nicked his ribs. Using every ounce of his strength, Tahoka squeezed the brave's face with his massive fingers as he held on to the wrist with his free hand.

Twisting the sentry's wrist until the knife fell from his grip, Tahoka head-butted the man with so much force that he felt his own knees buckle.

The brave went limp.

Tahoka lowered the unconscious Indian to the ground and removed the blanket from the man's shoulders. He wrapped it around himself and stood staring out into the darkness. He could feel blood trickling from the wound on his side but knew the bleeding would soon stop. He never bled for long however severe the wounds.

The hundred or so warriors nearby had neither seen nor heard a thing.

Soon he knew the scent of the sentry had attached itself to him and he felt confident enough to move closer to the ponies. As he walked through the midst of the hundred or more mounts, none gave him a second glance as they continued eating. The smell of the blanket was known to their sensitive nostrils.

Tahoka was now a mere twenty feet from one of the camp-fires and could hear the dozen braves' conversation clearly. He sat down, lowered his head and listened.

Soon, he prayed, he would hear the braves talking about why they were here, holding siege to the mission. All Tahoka had to do was wait and he would discover the truth.

All Tahoka had to do was wait.

FIFTEEN

The only room which remained reasonably habitable within the old mission offered little comfort to Judge Holmes and Clara King as they sat silently staring at the unconscious scout. Darkness had brought even more fear into the heaving bosom of the beautiful Clara King as she sat opposite the rotund figure of Judge Holmes who still remained close to his strongbox.

Illuminated by the stagecoach lanterns, the room still retained more shadows than places where eyes could focus with any true certainty.

The four walls of the large room appeared animated as the lantern light flickered hauntingly. Earlier Clara had watched as Salty Sagebrush fought to stem the flow of blood from the wound in Tate Morse's leg. Perhaps it had been the first time in her short life that her innocent eyes had seen such a gory wound.

Even now, as Clara sat alone on the long wooden bench away from the others, her back pressed up against the wall, her heart raced as her shocked mind tried to understand the nightmare she found herself in.

This was meant to be a return home after visiting her estranged father at Mission Wells. Now there seemed little chance of ever leaving this place alive. The sight of so much blood in such a short period of time had torn away her once boundless courage.

Now she was shaking with terror as her imagination filled her thoughts with a thousand horrifying images. Each one worse than the one before.

Across the wide room Judge Holmes had remained close to his strongbox, silently trying to maintain his belief in the fact that they would soon be saved from this horror. Yet as the day's light had evaporated and blackness had silently overwhelmed the mission, even Holmes began to doubt that anything good could result from this situation.

There were simply too many Apaches out there and too few able-bodied men within the walls of the old mission. Even though Major Lincoln had ridden out for help, it was doubtful that the overweight cavalry officer would reach the troopers he sought. If Lincoln had remained he at least might have known how to defend against attack.

Holmes knew that if he had travelled only twelve hours earlier, he would now be sitting in his favourite saloon, drinking their best brandy and trying to decide which girl to invite up to his room.

Tate Morse lay as still as a corpse on one of the long benches where Sagebrush had left him after saving his life. For hours the old scout had simply slept unaware of anything or anyone around him.

Boyce Lee and his partner, Reno, silently entered the room, carrying both their saddle-bags. They felt the eyes of Clara and Holmes suddenly drawn to them.

Both men seemed nervous. Yet theirs was a very different kind of fear which had nothing to do with the warriors beyond the mission walls. They had something planned.

Lee glanced across to Reno and then at the seductive strongbox near the judge. Both men nodded knowingly to one another as they moved deeper into the cool room.

Holmes lifted his head and watched as the pair paused half-way into the cavernous area.

'You boys got any food in them bags?'

Reno glanced angrily at the banker and spat at the seated figure. A man whose shape bore witness to the fact that he had missed very few large meals during his lifetime drew nothing but contempt from the lean figure.

'If we had grub, we sure wouldn't give any to a fat bastard like you.'

'Damn right.' Lee nodded in agreement, pushed his Stetson off his face and looked at the silent female sitting close to the wall.

'I'd share with her though,' Reno smiled as his eyes focused on Clara – huddled on the bench against the wall.

'Me too. I'd give her anything she wants.' Boyce Lee found himself chuckling as his mind was taken away from their chosen objective.

Reno grinned in agreement and followed his partner towards the quiet Clara King.

'Reckon she might taste better than an inch-thick T-bone steak, Boyce,' Lee said, licking his lips as he began to sense her perfume in his nostrils.

'She's probably never been tasted before, partner. We could be the first.' Lee raised his right leg and rested his boot upon Clara's dress, pinning it to the bench. Before she had time to say anything, Reno sat down on the opposite side.

'There ain't nothing like fresh meat.'

'You said it, partner.'

If nothing else could bring her confused brain out of the shocked state it had found itself in, the smell of the two men filling her nostrils did.

Suddenly they were all over her.

As the lantern light flickered eerily around the

room, she found it impossible to focus on either man's face.

'How much?' Lee asked quietly trying to ensure his words found only her ears.

Clara looked up at the face which was bathed in shadow.

'I don't understand. How much is what?'

Reno moved an inch closer until he could feel her thigh touching his own.

'You ain't shy, is you?'

For one desperate moment she tried to stand but found her dress pinned down on both sides by the two men. As the filthy left hand of the younger man reached across and touched her chin, Clara King realized what real fear was.

'Please go away,' Clara said in a hushed tone as if it would be an admission of some sort of forbidden knowledge if she spoke loud enough to alert the elderly banker of her plight.

'Easy, honey. Me and Reno know how to pleasure a lady.' Lee oozed his words like a rattler releasing its venom.

As panic began to race through her entire body, the innocent beauty tried to work out what she ought to do.

Should she scream?

Fight?

Claw at their faces with her long fingernails?

Perhaps they were just teasing her. Maybe men

out in the wilderness did this sort of thing without meaning any true harm.

'You sure is a looker, girl,' Reno said, holding her chin in his strong fingers. Her eyes flashed between his image and that of the standing Boyce Lee.

'Eh, thank you,' Clara said, trying to pull her face back from his evil-smelling fingers.

'You must be pretty expensive if your clothes are anything to go by,' Lee said, allowing one of his own hands to feel the quality of the fabric which covered her body.

'I'll give you a golden eagle.' Reno sighed as he leaned even closer to the terrified woman.

'Why?' Clara asked.

'Just hitch up them petticoats, girl,' Lee said, gripping her hair with his left hand whilst letting his right rest on her covered knee.

Clara King's eyes widened as her worst fears became reality.

'I'll scream,' she warned.

Lee shook his head. 'Screaming out will only make me and the boy angry, girl. You got a mouth of real fine teeth and I'd hate for you to lose any of them.'

Reno unbuckled his gunbelt and laid it down on the bench at his side before starting to undo the buttons on his pants.

'No!' Clara exclaimed, trying to break free.

'You can't refuse before you done seen the merchandise, missy,' Reno grunted, fumbling inside his long johns.

Judge Holmes rose from the bench opposite and walked towards the scene which even he found impossible to ignore.

'I think you have frightened the little lady enough, men.'

Boyce Lee smiled as he glanced into the eyes of his partner and then the girl. He used the fingers of his right hand to work the long dress up over her knees.

Holmes stood directly behind Lee and cleared his throat several times until Lee slowly turned to face him.

'Go and sit down, old man,' Boyce Lee commanded, his fingers continuing to work the material up.

'I shall go and inform the others if you don't quit that,' Judge Holmes announced.

Before the banker had moved a single pace away from the bench he felt a sudden blow to his back. For a brief moment Holmes imagined he had just been punched. It was only as he turned to complain that he saw the blade in Lee's fist glistening in the lantern-light.

As he began to open his mouth, Holmes felt the horror within his body and noticed the blood dripping from the razor-sharp knife. Suddenly his

112

mouth was filled with blood and he felt himself staggering towards the three figures.

Holmes gasped as he hit the floor, and tried to crawl back to his strongbox. Death stopped the banker swiftly.

Lee slid the knife back into his tall boot, and returned his hand to Clara's knees.

As she stared down at the hand, Clara could see the blood on her clothing. Holmes's blood.

Before she could scream out the hand covered her mouth, almost choking her as it pressed hard into her face. She could taste the blood as her eyes stared into the crazed pupils of Boyce Lee.

'Ya know something?' Lee sighed.

'What?' Reno responded.

'I figure you can keep the golden eagle.'

'I was going to anyway. We only pay whores; this gal ought to be paying us.'

Both men laughed as they concentrated on their captive.

Clara King felt the buttons which started at her neck and ceased at her waist being ripped from her dress by their hands as they kept her pinned to the wall. She was struggling, yet they had her where they wanted her. No matter how much strength she tried to muster, it was not enough. Not against the power of this evil pair.

Then she felt herself being turned on the bench by their forceful hands. Suddenly she was no longer sitting but lying upon the wooden bench. Its cold surface chilled her spine as she realized the top of her once pristine dress had been pulled completely from her upper body.

Lee's mouth began to bite at the pale flesh like a dog trying to tear meat from a bone.

Then Reno bore down on her, his mouth frantically seeking and finding her exposed breasts. Now both crazed men were almost fighting over her skin as if in contest with one another. She felt the cold chill of the evening air touching her legs and thighs as her under garments were stripped from her lower body.

Boyce Lee's unshaven stubble scraped her flesh, making her arch in agony. Then she felt the last of her clothing being torn from her legs and tried vainly to kick out at her attackers.

If only she could free her mouth from the filthy sweat-soaked hand long enough to scream for help, she thought, would any of the other men come to her assistance or would they line up behind Reno and Lee and await their turn?

The image of the smiling Mexican bandit came into her mind as she moved her head back and forth trying to free herself of the strong suffocating hand.

Zococa would help her.

Or would he?

Finally as she bucked and twisted upon the

bench she managed to free her face long enough to take in enough air to scream.

'Zococa!' Clara bellowed.

Suddenly the blade of the knife, still wet with the banker's blood, was placed across her abdomen. She could feel its sharp edge ready to cut her life from her body.

Clara stopped kicking as the cold steel was pressed into her skin just hard enough to warn her not to resist any more.

The hand was pressed into her face again. She vainly searched for air enough to fill her lungs. As teeth found her nipples and an unaccustomed weight pressed down upon her hips, Clara King began to sink into a place where demons reigned.

Had her scream to the handsome bandit been entirely in vain?

SIXTEEN

'If you do not stop, I shall surely kill you,' Zococa said in a slow, deliberate tone. There was no question that he meant it.

Boyce Lee turned his head and raised himself off the helpless Clara King. Reno had slumped to the floor, where he tried frantically to hitch his pants back up. Both men were angry because they had not done what they intended to do with the female. They had been interrupted and for that, the Mexican bandit had to pay.

Lee's eyes narrowed as he slowly did up his trouser buttons whilst keeping his back to the Mexican.

'Big talk for a dude Mex. What do you think, Reno?' Lee announced loudly as he stared down at his gunbelt lying between the naked legs of the bruised and battered female. There was no chance of reaching it without being shot but Lee, as always, had a plan.

116

'Yeah, Boyce. Mighty big talk,' Reno agreed, keeping watch on Zococa's every movement.

'Move away from the lady, *amigos*,' Zococa ordered. His thumb pulled the hammer of his silver-plated pistol back until it fully locked.

Lee was holding the large knife in his left hand as the fingers on his right finally fastened the last of his pants' buttons. His eyes darted down at Reno's face and he silently mouthed for his partner to get ready to use the guns on the bench behind his head.

Reno nodded, secured his own belt and then stared through the legs of his partner at the tall Mexican bandit. Zococa made an ominous sight even to the most hardened of gunfighters. For, when holding his prized pistol, he did not smile.

'Turn around, *amigo*,' Zococa ordered.

'You figure on killing unarmed men, Zococa?' Boyce Lee asked. He turned the knife around in his fingers until he was holding the bloodstained blade firmly.

'Turn around or I shall kill you where you stand, Señor Lee.' Zococa's voice held no humour as he stepped closer to the pair of evil men. The bandit had spotted the body of Judge Holmes as soon as he had entered the large room with its pitifully inadequate lantern-light. It had taken a few seconds longer for him to notice the form of Clara King beneath the villainous pair.

Her desperate scream had brought him here as soon as he had heard it ringing on the cold night air. As he aimed his pistol in Lee's direction, Zococa found it increasingly hard not to pull the trigger.

Zococa wanted to kill both men like the vermin they were.

He wanted them dead.

Never before had he felt such anger filling his mind as he wondered whether or not he was too late to save the young lady. This, mixed with the fear of what might have happened to Tahoka at the hands of the Apaches, chilled Zococa.

Reno rose on to one knee. He watched the approaching bandit, keenly waiting for his chance to reach for his guns on the bench beside Clara's head.

As Clara moved her arms and tried to cover her naked torso with her small hands, Zococa sighed with relief.

She was alive, he thought.

'Is that you, Zococa?' Clara King gasped, suddenly realizing that it was the Mexican who had stopped Lee and Reno from finishing what they had started.

Before Zococa could return any words to the young woman, Boyce Lee swung around quickly.

Even in the flickering light of the stagecoach lanterns, Zococa was able to catch a brief glimpse of the metal blade as it left Lee's hand and hurtled towards him. He threw himself to his right and felt a sharp pain in his left hand as the knife struck the gun from his grip.

Zococa crashed to the ground and rolled over across the floor, upturning one of the lanterns and spilling flaming oil in a large pool. Before he had managed to get back to his feet he saw both men clawing at their weapons, trying to get a bead on him in the dancing light.

As he threw himself over the rising flames in the direction of his pistol where it lay on the floor, Zococa knew that he had only one chance of grabbing his weapon. To fail would leave him defenceless against the pair of gunmen who had already started to fire across the room in his direction.

As Zococa's left hand gripped his gun a bullet tore his wide-brimmed sombrero from his head. Without bothering to aim, the bandit returned fire instinctively.

The sound of Reno's voice screaming out in agony as two of Zococa's bullets hit him echoed around the large room. Zococa threw himself down behind one of the numerous benches as a volley of bullets from Boyce Lee's weapons ripped massive chunks of wood off its edge.

For an instant Zococa thought it would be only a matter of seconds before his own deadly accuracy would kill the arrogant Lee.

Then everything altered. The Mexican heard the pained voice of Clara King shrieking as Boyce Lee dragged her naked body up from the bench to use as a shield.

'Help me, Zococa. Help me,' came her cries.

After replacing his spent shells with new ones, Zococa crawled to the end of the bench and rose to his feet once more. He was shocked to see Clara's perfect form being used to protect Lee. He cocked the hammer into place again, then hesitated whilst Lee moved backward towards the open doorway with his hostage.

With each step, Clara screamed out for help – help that Zococa was unable to give. As he raised his pistol and tried to aim, he realized that the swaying light and the monstrous shadows gave no certainty even to a marksman such as himself, as to where his bullets might go.

Sweat ran down his temples as Zococa stared along the barrel of his pistol at the forms bathed in flickering lantern-light.

To fire would be foolhardy.

Zococa had played many games in his life but never at the expense of an innocent victim. As Lee fired at him again the bandit could do nothing but watch.

Then he heard the sound of a gun-hammer being locked into place to his left. Swinging around on his knees, he saw Reno propped up against a wall holding his pistol at arm's length. The two bullet holes in his belly had soaked his pants in blood yet somehow he refused to die just yet.

The gun was aimed straight at Zococa's midriff.

As the injured man squeezed his trigger a cloud of acrid smoke bellowed between them. A white-hot flash traced the path of the bullet. As the bullet passed within an inch of his face the sound of the shot deafened Zococa.

The bandit fired one single bullet into Reno's head. His body drooped over, lifeless, until the skull crashed on to the floor. Zococa crouched down, waiting for Boyce Lee to open up again.

As his eyes glanced to the doorway, Zococa realized the man had gone. He had taken Clara King with him.

The Mexican rose from his place of cover and raced across the room to the doorway. Again Clara's scream for help and mercy rang out somewhere in the darkness of the mission's courtyard.

As he was about to venture out into the black night, two bullets blasted into the wall, sending dust into Zococa's face and stopping him in his tracks.

For a moment, Zococa was blinded.

Bending over, Zococa tried to rub the dust from his eyes as he listened to the sound of footsteps. One set was coming towards him whilst another was heading away.

'Zococa! What's going on?'

'What's all the shooting about?'

'You OK?'

As the tall bandit cleared his eyes enough to be able to see again, he recognized the voices to his right.

He leaned on the wall and said nothing as his burning eyes tried to see where Boyce Lee had gone with his hostage. There could be only one place, he reckoned.

The stables.

'What's happening?' Salty Sagebrush asked, reaching the silent bandit who just stared out into the darkness.

Zococa glanced at he faces of Josh Willis and Charlie Higgs, then looked down into the bearded features of the stagecoach driver.

'Lee has taken the beautiful lady, *amigo*.'

Willis stepped inside the large room where the carnage was still illuminated by the dying flames and the remaining lantern.

'Is they dead, Zococa?'

'*Sí*. They are very much dead,' Zococa replied, trying to think of some reason for all this. However hard he tried, he failed.

It just did not make sense.

'You kill them?' Higgs questioned wearily.

'I only killed Reno,' Zococa admitted. Then he heard the sound of horses being disturbed in the dark stables. The sound drew him away from the three men and he walked slowly towards the stables.

'Where you heading, boy?' Sagebrush asked.

Zococa did not reply.

SEVENTEEN

Zococa was only a dozen steps from the open door of the stables when he heard the voice of Boyce Lee booming out from the dark interior. In any other circumstances the handsome bandit would have charged in, firing his trusty Colt with little or no thought for his own safety. But not this night, with Clara King somewhere in the dark shadows. For all Zococa knew she was still being used as Lee's coat of armour.

'Stop right there, Zococa,' the voice ordered.

Zococa dropped on to one knee and rested his silver pistol against his chest, trying vainly to see into the darkness in hopes that he might get a glimpse of his target.

'I hear you, *amigo*. Do not harm the little lady.'

'You ain't gonna see this little filly alive again unless you do exactly as I tell you,' Lee shouted out from his perfect hiding place.

The sound of Clara King sobbing filled the bandit's ears and he felt his mouth going dry as he searched for words which might not cause the crazed gunman to do something deadly.

'I understand, *señor*,' Zococa called back. 'I am listening to you. Tell me what it is you wish me to do.'

'If you do exactly as I tell you, Zococa, you'll get the girl and I'll get what I want,' Lee called out his answer.

Zococa rose and moved cautiously a few paces to his left before speaking again. He was still not sure whether Lee could see him and was just waiting to get a clear shot.

'Tell me what you wish and I shall try to comply,' Zococa shouted towards the stables as he heard the horses becoming even more agitated.

'I could kill you right now, Zococa.' Lee began to laugh. The sound sent fear racing through the bandit as he wondered just how trustworthy Lee was. He had already proved himself to be an animal but would Lee keep his side of the bargain? Would he allow Clara to go free?

Zococa doubted it, yet had no option but to comply. Any other course of action would bring certain death to Clara King.

'What is it you wish Zococa to do?' the bandit asked, feeling sweat running down his temples and dripping off his jaw.

There was a long pause before Lee spoke again. 'You'll get my saddle-bags and the strongbox and bring them to me. Then I shall take one of the horses and ride out of here. Your pinto stallion looks the best of the bunch. I'll take it and the goods.'

'You will take my stallion?' Zococa asked.

'Would that upset you?'

'*Sí, señor*. It is a very fine animal.'

'Then I'll take your stallion.'

Zococa shook his head as his brain raced. 'But what of the Indians? They will be most hard to evade.'

'I figure your pinto can outrun any of them half-starved Apache ponies,' Lee growled.

'And what of the little lady?' Zococa questioned, moving even closer to the stable building. 'You will allow her to go unharmed if I bring you these things?'

'If you do as I told you, I'll leave the filly here unharmed.'

Zococa felt his heart racing even faster.

'I fear you will not keep your word, Señor Lee.'

'I can shoot her now and you and me can have an old-fashioned showdown,' Boyce Lee raged. 'Is that what you want?'

'I shall do as you say, *señor*.' Zococa sighed and knew he was not in any position to bargain with Lee. Lee had all the poker chips and it was his

126

pot. You cannot bluff a man with four aces, he thought.

'Do it fast,' Boyce Lee's voice snapped. 'I wanna be out of here a long time before dawn.'

'I will try to be as quick as possible.'

Zococa turned and headed back to the three waiting figures. As he came closer to the trio of anxious faces he began to wonder again about the saddle-bags, one of which Lee and Reno had not allowed out of their sight since reaching the mission. What could be so precious?

Zococa walked past the waiting men into the large room, then stopped and took several deep breaths. Once more his thoughts drifted to his friend Tahoka. Why had the giant Apache not yet returned? There were only two possible answers to the question. The mute Indian was either alive and waiting to discover reasons for his fellow Apaches being on the warpath or he had been captured and was already dead out there beyond the dunes.

'You looks a leetle bit worried, boy,' Sagebrush observed. He walked up to the troubled Mexican who stood silently next to the glowing lantern.

'I figured you would rush in there with your gun blazing, Zococa,' Josh Willis said.

'Zococa ain't that dumb.' Higgs spat as he patted the broad-shouldered bandit. 'He knew if he did that the girl would have been killed for sure.'

127

'What's eating you, boy?' Sagebrush asked the tall bandit. 'What iz you thinking about?'

Zococa's eyes looked into those of the bearded old man. His was a face a man could trust, unlike so many others he had seen over the years.

'There is something in one of those saddle-bags, *amigo*. Something Lee wants very badly.'

Sagebrush stepped over the bloody corpse of Judge Holmes and stared long and hard at the seemingly innocent bags which rested on the ground next to the bench.

'Should I take a looksee?'

Zococa swallowed hard, then nodded.

The room was completely silent as the old stage-coach driver's fingers carefully undid the buckles on the bags and pulled up both leather flaps.

'Oh my dear Lord,' Sagebrush gasped. He stepped nervously away from the bags and rested his ancient rear on the wooden seating.

'What is it?' Higgs asked.

'You look like you done seen a ghost, Salty,' Josh Willis pronounced. He approached the saddle-bags and bent down to lift the flaps. 'What's in here, anyway?'

'Don't look, Josh. Don't look,' Sagebrush pleaded.

Josh Willis paused. It was as if he were being warned, he thought.

'What's wrong, Salty?' Willis asked. He turned to face the old man.

Zococa brushed past Willis's shoulder and gazed into the face of the bearded man. As their eyes met, it was as if Sagebrush was telling him to beware of what his eyes were about to see.

Zococa leaned over and lifted the leather bag's flap and looked down into one of its deep pockets. Even he had not expected anything so utterly disgusting as the sight which met his eyes. Zococa let the large flap drop down again, then straightened up and turned to the three men.

None of them had seen the Mexican looking so pale before and only Sagebrush knew why Zococa looked so horrified.

'What's in that damned bag?' Josh Willis asked. He stepped forward until Zococa's outstretched hand stopped him in his tracks.

'It is best you never know, my friend,' Zococa said. He walked across the room and lifted the strongbox off the floor.

'How come?' Josh looked at Sagebrush innocently. 'What could be so bad?'

'You ever had a nightmare, Josh?' the old man asked.

Willis nodded.

'That's what's in the saddle-bag, young 'un.' Sagebrush hoisted himself off the bench and rubbed his toothless mouth along his sleeve. He gave the bag a wide berth.

'A nightmare?'

'Some men stoop lower than a sidewinder's belly.' Salty Sagebrush sighed and led the younger stagecoach man away from the saddle-bags. 'Some men can do things which can turn the guts of grown critters like me and Zococa.'

'I still don't get it,' Willis persisted as Zococa rested the heavy strongbox down beside the three men and tried to get his breath back. 'What's in them bags?'

'Hopefully you will never know, *amigo*,' Zococa answered. He looked out across the courtyard into the blackness where only noises dwelled.

EIGHTEEN

Josh Willis ran quickly across the courtyard carrying his Winchester back towards the mission entrance. He had two instructions: the first was to keep a keen eye out for Tahoka's return, and the second was to bring Clara King's large canvas bag back to the building where dead men rested in the dim lantern light.

The Mexican watched the young stagecoach guard until his burly figure disappeared into the darkness.

'How come you wanted Josh to bring her bag back, boy?' Salty Sagebrush asked curiously.

'She will require clothes, *amigo*,' Zococa said coldly. He wondered whether he would be able to save the beautiful female from the clutches of Boyce Lee. The way things were shaping up, it was doubtful that either of them would survive once Lee got his hands upon the strongbox and saddle-bags.

Zococa turned to Charlie Higgs and Sagebrush. His face was grim as he hauled the heavy strong-box off the floor and allowed the stagecoach driver to place the bulging saddle-bags carefully over his shoulder.

'You better be a leetle bit careful, Zococa,' Sagebrush told the young Mexican. 'That varmint will kill you if'n you give him half a chance.'

'Señor Lee is dealing the cards, *amigo*.' Zococa swallowed hard as he balanced the weight of his burden evenly.

'Then you better have yourself something hidden up your sleeve, Zococa,' Higgs interrupted. He slid a thin-bladed knife up the bandit's left jacket-sleeve, point first.

'Thank you, my friend,' Zococa whispered. He walked away from the two men. 'With any luck I may get a chance to use it.'

Charlie Higgs watched as the bandit continued to walk slowly towards the stables. Then he turned to Sagebrush and asked the question which had been burning in his craw for what seemed an eternity.

'I gotta know. What was in them bags, Salty?'

'A sacred Apache necklace, Charlie,' Sagebrush said quietly. 'I figure Lee and Reno must have stolen it a leetle while before I picked them up on the mountain trail.'

'You and Zococa got mighty fired up over a mere

necklace,' Higgs said. 'I thought you was gonna spew up in there.'

Sagebrush shook as a chill overwhelmed his ancient bones.

'It weren't the necklace that turned my old guts, Charlie.'

'Then what?' Higgs scratched his chin and stared at the white beard that hid most of Sagebrush's face.

For a moment Sagebrush did nothing but listen to the sound of Zococa's spurs tinkling as he walked on towards the stables. Then he looked round at the bemused scout.

'And?' Higgs pressed.

'There was the head of an Apache girl attached to it, Charlie.'

Josh Willis struck a match, cupped the flame in his hands and studied the baggage-labels beneath the canvas flap of the stagecoach's tail-gate. He had no idea why Zococa wanted the female's baggage but knew there must be a good reason. Just as he had recognized a luggage-tag with the name of Clara King on it and was about to drag the heavy bag out, a hand suddenly rested upon his shoulder.

Willis dropped the match and then knocked his Winchester over as the firm grip turned him around on his heels. For one cruel tortuous moment he imagined his life was over and he expected a tomahawk to come crashing down on to his skull. Yet death did not come, only the grunting of a huge exhausted man.

Josh Willis tried desperately to see who was holding him in check. Then, as the guard's vision adjusted to the darkness he recognized the giant Apache who towered over even his impressive height.

In the faint light of the stars, Josh Willis knew the features of Tahoka.

Willis rolled his eyes heavenward in relief, and rested his back against the body of the coach. His heart was beating at twice its normal rate as at last he managed to force words from his dry mouth.

'Thank the Lord it's you, Tahoka. I thought you was one of them other Apaches. You scared the hell out of me. I thought I was a goner.'

The Indian grunted and shook Willis's shoulder until he had his total attention. There was an urgency in the eyes of the Apache which perplexed the guard. Tahoka was desperately trying to tell him something and was furious with himself that he could not communicate.

'I don't understand,' Willis said as Tahoka released his grip and turned his huge frame towards the dim light where Sagebrush and Charlie Higgs could still be seen. 'I ain't as smart as your pal Zococa. I can't read your hands like he does.'

Tahoka nodded vigorously and pointed excitedly at the building where men were moving about in front of the lantern illumination.

'Yeah. That's where Zococa is. Down there with the boys,' Josh Willis said.

The massive Indian set off at a run towards the men. Josh grabbed hold of the canvas bag from the stage tail-gate and then started after Tahoka.

NINETEEN

'Hold it just about there, Zococa,' Boyce Lee said coldly from somewhere within the depths of the stables. The shadows were still protecting him.

Zococa stopped walking when he heard the words.

'I have done as you told me, *amigo*. I bring everything you told me. Now can the little lady go free?'

'I'll tell you when.' Lee's voice seemed to fade away as the words reached the bandit. The sound of movement inside the dark stable caused the hair on his neck to rise as Zococa tried to work out where the footsteps of Lee were headed. Holding the heavy strongbox was almost as much as he could do, but with the extra weight of the saddle-bags upon his shoulder, Zococa began to feel every muscle in his lean frame starting to buckle.

'May I put this down?'

'Sure,' Lee's voice answered.

'Thank you, *amigo*.'

'Just remember that my gun is aimed right at your heart.'

Zococa slowly bent his knees and lowered the strongbox to the ground before letting the bags slip from his shoulder. The bandit strained his eyes trying to locate the vicious killer.

'You done good for an ignorant Mexican,' Boyce Lee sneered. Suddenly he appeared from Zococa's right and placed the barrel of his pistol against the bandit's neck. Zococa could not understand how the man had appeared from the direction totally opposite to that from which the sound had emanated.

'Bravo, Señor Lee. This I did not expect.' Zococa screwed up his eyes to see what had made the sound which he had taken for Lee. Then he made out the unmistakable outline of the naked woman tied to a wooden upright just inside the stable opening.

'You are going to kill the great Zococa?' the bandit asked, feeling his blood starting to boil in his veins.

Lee pushed the gun-barrel deeper into the neck of the kneeling bandit.

'Not yet. There are a few things we gotta do first.'

Zococa managed to rise slowly to his full height. The cold metal of the gun-barrel remained against his neck just below his ear. It was only the feel of the cold steel which kept the bandit from exploding in anger.

'You confuse me, *señor*. What is it you wish of me?'

'Quit gabbing, Zococa,' Lee snarled.

'*Sí, amigo*. I quit gabbing,' Zococa said, keeping his hands raised.

'I want you to shoot the lock off that strongbox,' Lee said. He moved behind the Mexican, keeping the gun-barrel pressed against the younger man's head.

'But it is very dark. I could end up shooting a hole in my foot.' Zococa forced himself to laugh as he found his eyes adjusting at last to the lack of light.

'The stories I heard about you tell of a bandit who can shoot a cigarette from a man's mouth, Zococa.' Lee pushed the gun barrel hard into the nape of Zococa's neck.

'I have also heard these stories, *amigo*.' Carefully Zococa lowered his left arm, ensuring that the secreted knife remained firmly trapped between his shirt and jacket sleeve.

'Careful, Zococa,' Lee warned. 'You shoot the lock off the box and then you drop your gun on to the ground. Understand?'

'I understand.' Zococa continued lowering his arm until his fingers hovered over the grip of the silver-plated pistol. Then he slowly pulled the weapon free of its holster and slid his index finger across the trigger. He wanted to turn and kill Boyce Lee but knew even he was not fast enough to stop a bullet from entering the back of his head.

Zococa had to do as he was told for a while longer, however much it angered him.

'Easy now. Remember, you only shoot the lock off the strongbox.' Boyce Lee pushed the barrel of his own gun into the black hair of the bandit, making sure there would be no heroics..

Pulling the hammer of his gun back until it locked into place, Zococa lowered the pistol until it was aiming at the large metal box at his feet.

'This is not an easy shot in the darkness, my friend.'

'You got six shells to get it right, Zococa,' Lee said firmly as he rested his own Colt against the back of the bandit's head.

Zococa bit his lower lip as sweat trickled down his face, and aimed at the box. His eyes were still not fully adjusted to the darkness inside the stable.

Squeezing the trigger, Zococa felt the weapon kick as it spat out a bullet. The sound was deafening but also informative. Both men heard the sound of the padlock shattering into a dozen pieces as the bright flash lit up the stable for a brief instant.

Kicking at the box, Zococa confirmed that his shot had indeed done the job and then carefully dropped the gun onto the ground as he had been instructed.

'A darn good shot, Zococa,' Lee said, pushing the taller man forward into the shadows before opening the lid of the strongbox and inspecting its contents.

Zococa steadied himself then he noticed the shivering Clara King leaning upon the wooden upright to which she was tethered like a dog.

'Do not be afraid, senorita. Soon Zococa will make you free.'

Before she could reply, Boyce Lee growled again as he scooped up Zococa's prized silver-plated pistol from the ground before discarding his own.

'Just thought you might wanna know that my gun is empty.'

Zococa nodded. 'You are indeed a very brave man, *señor*. To face Zococa with an empty pistol is something most men would not have the nerve to do.'

Lee pointed at the ground next to Zococa's feet.

'I took your empty saddle-bags off your pinto, Zococa. There they are waiting for you to fill with the money from that fat juicy strongbox. Now get to work.'

Zococa turned his head and managed to see his own empty bags on the ground in the shadows.

Stooping down he picked them up and stepped close to the open box. He dropped on to his knees and started to transfer the coins into it.

'You are a very smart man, Señor Lee,' Zococa said. He tilted his head slightly as the familiar sound of an owl filled his ears. Zococa knew that Tahoka had returned and was signalling to him from somewhere within the walls of the mission. The huge Indian might not be able to speak but he could impersonate almost every bird along the border.

Boyce Lee kicked sand over the kneeling Mexican. 'Just fill them bags.'

Zococa did as he was told, yet with every handful of coins he dropped into the leather pockets of the saddle-bags, he knew his own life was getting shorter unless Tahoka could distract the gunman.

There was little point in Boyce Lee allowing him to live after he had completed his task and Zococa knew it. He wondered where his Apache friend was. Zococa knew the huge warrior could move undetected right up to an enemy without them ever hearing a single footstep.

Yet even Tahoka was not as fat as a bullet and if Lee squeezed on the trigger of the silver Colt, death would come instantly to the Mexican bandit.

That was the only certainty in all this.

Zococa buckled the first pocket securely and

then turned the black leather bag around and started filling the second deep pocket with coins.

'Faster,' Lee snarled. He pulled the gun hammer back until it locked.

'Please let us go. You have what you wanted.' Clara King's pitiful voice sobbed, causing both men to glance in her direction.

'This is true, *amigo*. You could let us go and ...'

'You killed Reno and the Bible says "an eye for an eye", Zococa,' Lee growled down at the kneeling bandit.

'He was going to kill me,' Zococa observed.

'Because you spoiled our little bit of fun,' Lee said peevishly as he moved closer to the Mexican. 'You're only jealous because we got to the filly first.'

'There is a big difference between you and me when it comes to the pretty ladies, *señor*.' Zococa sighed. 'The women beg you to stop but they beg me to start.'

Zococa could feel the knife in his sleeve but wondered if he would get a chance to use it. Then he heard the sound of an owl hooting again. Tahoka was now close.

This time the sound made Boyce Lee raise the weapon in his hand and look around the array of shadows which surrounded them.

'You hear that?'

'*Sí, señor*,' Zococa replied. He let the stiletto

slide down his sleeve into his left hand. This time, the darkness was on his side, as it masked the deadly weapon from the haunted eyes of Lee. 'It was only an owl, I think.'

'Could be them Apaches are starting to get a tad braver,' Lee muttered.

'Indians do not attack at night.'

Lee looked down at the bandit. 'Are you sure?'

'Not exactly, *amigo*.' Zococa dropped the last of the coins into the saddle-bag pocket and buckled it up. 'Tell me one thing?'

Lee seemed unaware that Zococa had completed his task. He strained his eyes, trying to locate where the owl call had come from. 'What ya wanna know?'

'Why is there the head of an Apache girl in your own saddle-bags?'

Lee lowered his head until he was staring down at the kneeling figure.

'You opened our bags?'

'Reluctantly I did so.' Zococa felt the slim knife-blade between his fingers and toyed with it as he watched the man above him moving closer.

'Well, we didn't intend cutting off her head but one thing led to another and Reno kinda went loco.' Lee sighed as he kicked his own saddle-bags holding the horrific prize. 'We was hired by a certain party to get hold of certain sacred Apache artefacts. We managed to trade our way into the main camp and did a lot of business until we located the necklace hanging about the neck of the daughter of Chief Hezonimo.'

'Hezonimo?' Zococa had heard the name even south of the border.

'Yeah. He allowed us to pitch our bedrolls in his camp overnight and that was our chance to steal the necklace.' Lee seemed to be relieved to be getting the whole sordid story off his chest. 'Reno had been giving the girl the eye all day making her think he liked her. So when the sun set she slipped out to be with him. Reno weren't no sweet-talker and made a move for the necklace too darn quick. She got scared and started to try and call out so he slit her throat.'

Zococa shook his head as he listened to the story unfolding.

'Then Reno panicked,' Boyce Lee continued. 'With the chief's daughter dead he came to me and I tried to remove the necklace from her neck but it was tangled in her long hair. That piece of jewellery is worth a lot of money to the right folks back East and we weren't about to leave it there. For over an hour we tried to free the gold chain from her damn hair but it was impossible and we both knew it. I was for leaving it there but Reno had a better idea. Using the girl's own knife, he cut her head clean off.'

Zococa swallowed hard. 'What happened to your horses?'

'We managed to get clear of the camp but them redskins must have found her body faster than we planned. As we rode through the mountains just after dawn we ran into a small hunting party and all hell broke loose. We killed the bastards but they managed to do for our horses. Their ponies spooked so we grabbed our saddles and the saddle-bags and headed down to the trail which we knew the stage used.'

Both men suddenly heard the sound of an owl once more. As Lee swung around with the pistol in his hand, Zococa jumped to his feet.

Before the Mexican had time to throw the narrow-bladed knife he saw the massive figure of Tahoka flying though the air and hitting Lee off his feet. The gun exploded as the gunman hit the ground with the Apache on his chest.

The pistol fired into the air three times more as the two men wrestled on the ground in the darkness at Zococa's feet. Lee smashed the barrel of the weapon into the head of the warrior with all his strength but Tahoka refused to succumb. As the Apache rolled over on to his back he raised the lighter man into the air, making sure he continued to grip the hand holding the pistol as once more it fired into the night sky.

Then Tahoka raised his legs and began to squeeze at Boyce Lee's midriff. The more the gunman struggled, the more Tahoka increased his pressure until the sound of the man's back breaking echoed around the courtyard.

Boyce Lee seemed to shake uncontrollably as death overcame him and he slumped into the arms of the massive Indian.

For a moment Zococa had wondered if Tahoka needed help but then he saw how quickly his gigantic friend despatched the ruthless gunman.

As Tahoka rose to his feet he snatched the silver pistol from Lee's hand and tossed it to his partner who slipped it into his holster.

Both men looked at the sky above their heads.

Suddenly it was no longer black but coming alive with the golden rays of dawn. Both men looked at one another, then Tahoka began to speak to his friend with his hands. Zococa watched as his friend explained everything he had learned during his foray amongst the encamped Apache braves.

'This is bad, my little elephant. Very bad,' Zococa said. He turned to look at the tethered Clara. 'Go and get the little lady a dress from her bag and bring it back to me.'

Tahoka nodded and ran back towards the room where the other men waited.

Zococa ran to Clara, and used his knife to cut her bonds. Then he removed his jacket and wrapped it around her body, making sure his eyes did not dwell on her nakedness.

'Are we now safe, Zococa? Is it over?'

Zococa ran his index finger and thumb over his thin black moustache as he thought.

He did not reply because he did not know the answer. All he knew for sure was that it was not over yet. Tahoka had just told him that the body of Major Lincoln was lying dead beyond the sand dunes.

With the sun starting to rise, it might be only just beginning, he thought. Somehow he had to try and think of a way of ending this.

TWENTY

From the top of the high wall above the mission archway, Zococa stared across the arid sand towards the war-smoke which had begun to rise once more from beyond the dunes. It had been light for a mere ten minutes but already it was obvious that the distant Indians were ready to attack the mission.

The warriors were now ready to let themselves be seen in all their glory, as they rode confidently to the crest of the long sand dune.

Chief Hezonimo and his warriors sat silently atop their painted ponies watching the adobe edifice. They knew that they did not have to attack just yet. They were playing with the trapped occupants like a cat does with a mouse. Now they were content to allow fear to win the first round for them.

The Mexican bandit knew there was little time left to try and put an end to this. The silent line of nearly one hundred Apache braves said more than a thousand words could ever convey.

Sagebrush stayed beside Zococa, looking at the Indians and tried to work out if they had enough ammunition to fend off the braves.

'This is very serious, I think, *amigo*,' Zococa said dryly as he heard the other men climbing up to join them on the makeshift parapet.

'We ain't gonna hold them at bay for long,' Sagebrush sighed as he made room for the massive Tahoka whilst Higgs and Willis lay on their bellies holding two of the Winchester rifles a few feet away.

'Oh dear Lord,' Charlie Higgs muttered as he caught sight of the line of brightly coloured braves silently watching the old mission.

'I figure my wife is gonna be a widow real soon, Salty,' Josh Willis drawled. His trembling hands clutched at his carbine.

'She won't be a widow for long,' Sagebrush said.

'This all wrong,' Zococa said shaking his head. 'I am the great Zococa and I do not hide like a snivelling coward waiting to die.'

Tahoka breathed heavily through his wide nostrils and watched the line of warriors opposite the mission. They were dressed for battle. Time was running out faster than his companions realized and he knew it. The large man began to talk with his hands to Zococa once more.

Zococa read his partner's hands and fingers, taking in the frantic explosion of silent conversation.

'Enough, my little rhinoceros,' Zococa waved his hand in front of the stony face. 'I am getting the headache from all your chatter. I understand.'

Tahoka grunted.

'What's he going on about, Zococa?' Charlie Higgs asked curiously.

'My little one tells me that we have what Chief Hezonimo wants,' Zococa replied, running his fingers down his jawline thoughtfully. 'Perhaps if we can get it back to him, we might survive.'

'You mean the saddle-bag with the necklace in it?' Sagebrush turned and gripped his friend's arm. 'Does Tahoka reckon we could end this by letting them Apache have it back?'

Zococa looked hard into the face of his partner.

'Would this satisfy Hezonimo, Tahoka?'

Tahoka pursed his lips, considering the question carefully before speaking with his hands again.

Zococa read the words and raised an eyebrow.

'This I do not like, little one. This is very dangerous.'

Tahoka shrugged.

'What he say, Zococa?' Josh Willis asked.

'Has he got a plan?' Higgs added.

Sagebrush tried to restrain his own curiosity as

he watched the troubled face of the Mexican trying to make sense of Tahoka's suggestion.

'You look a leetle bit worried, boy. I figure our big friend here has come up with a real humdinger of a plan. But it don't sit well in your craw.'

Zococa sighed. '*Sí*, Señor Salty. Tahoka wants to take the saddle-bags to Chief Hezonimo. This is suicidal even for an Apache.'

Sagebrush considered the simple idea for quite a while, his old eyes staring out at the warriors facing them. Then, scratching his white beard, he began to speak.

'Them Indians ain't gonna go away whilst we got them saddle-bags in here, boy. Tahoka knows that. The trouble is, I figure they'll want more than just the bags to quit.'

Zococa leaned closer to the stagecoach driver.

'Continue, *amigo*. Zococa is most interested.'

'Reno and Lee.' Sagebrush spat out the names of the two men who had caused so much grief to all who had encountered them.

'What about them?' Zococa tilted his head and looked hard into the twinkling eyes of the old man. 'Did I not kill them already? Are they not dead? What good are they?'

Sagebrush raised his bushy eyebrows as a toothless smile crossed his face.

'Does them Apache know you killed them varmints?'

Tahoka looked at his partner's face. A face which was starting to smile once more.

Zococa looked at Tahoka and then Sagebrush. He burst out laughing and slapping his leg.

'Of course. Now I understand. They want Reno and Lee and the precious gift which was taken by them from the Apache camp. All we have to do is...?'

Tahoka rolled his eyes and sat upright. Seeing Zococa's face suddenly go blank, the huge Indian began to make hand signals once more.

'Exactly, my valiant one. This is what I was already thinking just before you gave me the headache by interrupting.' Zococa smiled broadly. 'But let us allow Sagebrush to have the honour of saying how he thinks we can execute this most simple plan.'

'We unhitch two more of the stagecoach team and then secure the bodies of Reno and Lee to them with the saddle-bags. Then we let them horses ride out of the gates for Hezonimo and his chums to follow.' Salty Sagebrush looked long and hard into the faces of the two men closest to him. 'Is that what you was gonna say, Zococa?'

'Word for word, *amigo*.' Zococa grinned and he patted the arm of his large friend Tahoka. 'Is this not a better plan than the one you had, my little one?'

Reluctantly, Tahoka nodded.

'What in tarnation are you men jabbering about?' Willis asked nervously.

'You and Charlie stay here and watch for them Apaches to start something.' Sagebrush pointed his finger at the youthful Josh Willis. 'And don't shoot any of them unless they shoots at you first.'

'OK, Salty. But I don't get it.' Willis sounded mystified. He looked at the equally puzzled Higgs.

Zococa rose first and began to descend from the wall down to the floor of the mission with Tahoka and Sagebrush right behind him.

Sagebrush and Zococa ran towards the stable to get the horses. Tahoka headed for the building to collect the body of Reno. As the large Indian entered the room his eyes caught sight of Clara King sitting in a new dress upon a bench next to the unconscious Tate Morse.

She looked up to the stone-faced man and saw the compassion in his face. Raising his hand to his heart he made a slow bowing gesture. Her gentle smile was accepted by the warrior with a nod. Then he dragged Reno's body through the doorway out into the courtyard.

FINALE

Zococa made sure the two bodies were well and truly secured to the backs of the mounts before throwing the saddle-bags over the neck of the mount holding Reno's body. Using a leather lace, his nimble fingers tied the bags around the neck of the dead bandit.

'Is that gonna do it?' Salty asked as he waddled up to them.

Tahoka raised a hand and then removed a small trinket from his long braided hair and tied this to the buckle of the saddle-bags.

'What is that, *amigo*?' Zococa questioned his friend.

Tahoka made a few gestures with his hands.

'It is something which Tahoka thinks his brother Apaches might be able to understand,' Zococa said as Sagebrush stared at the simple metal object hanging across the shoulder of the horse.

'I seen one of them things before,' the old-timer muttered as they began leading the two nervous animals toward the archway where the stage-coach had been moved just enough to allow the creatures to pass through.

'You have?' Zococa whispered curiously.

'It's meant to be big magic,' Sagebrush told him.

They slapped the tails of the two horses and the three men watched from beside the coach as the animals ran out into the blistering morning heat and raced away from the mission. Within seconds, the entire line of warriors rode down from the dunes and began to chase the galloping mounts.

'You boys might as well come down off that wall,' Sagebrush shouted to Willis and Higgs.

Zococa watched the two men coming down. He knew that they had played their best hand. Now if the Apaches were to return and still want to make war, there was little they could do.

'Now we have to wait a leetle longer, boys,' Sagebrush sighed.

'*Sí, amigo.* The battle may not have ended but we can pray.'

Tahoka tapped the shoulder of his partner. Zococa turned and stared at the figure of Clara King, who had watched their every move from the long dark shadows outside the room.

'I think that is a very pretty lady, Tahoka,' Zococa commented.

Tahoka nodded.

Charlie Higgs walked up to the tall Mexican. 'What's happening?'

'Go and check on Tate, Charlie,' Sagebrush suggested.

Higgs looked at the men. 'But what if they come back looking for scalps?'

'I'll let you know, darn fast,' Sagebrush assured him. He sighed and placed a hand on Josh Willis's shoulder.

'What you gonna do now, Salty?' the young guard asked.

'Hitch what's left of our team up to the stage-coach, boy.'

'Are we gonna try and leave here?'

Sagebrush pushed the man in the direction of the stable. 'We have to get out of here. We iz all a leetle bit hungry and there ain't no grub in this place. Indians or no Indians, we gotta make a break for it.'

Zococa stared out on to the desert plain and his heart began to race once more as he saw the Apache chief returning with his braves. This time they came within twenty yards of the mission before the chief reined in his pony.

There was a long silence as Hezonimo watched the three men who were standing next to the stagecoach. Tahoka stepped out into the sunshine and began to speak with his hands to the Apache chief. Then the warrior lifted his shield to the heavens and gave a haunting cry.

Zococa and Sagebrush watched in awe as the Apache swiftly rode back over the dune with the two coach-horses in tow. They had what they wanted.

'It is over, I think,' Zococa said, pushing his sombrero off his face.

'Sure is,' Sagebrush agreed. Tahoka walked silently back towards the men.

A little more than an hour later Charlie Higgs helped his friend Tate More towards the battered stagecoach.

'So you finally woked up, Tate,' Sagebrush chuckled from the driver's seat. He looked down on the men getting inside. 'A fat lot of use you was.'

Tate More looked up. 'Did I miss anything?'

Sagebrush shook his head.

'Just a leetle bit of trouble, that's all.'

Clara King moved hesitantly from the shadows on the arm of Zococa, whilst Tahoka carried the canvas bag. He handed it to Josh Willis, who was kneeling on the stagecoach roof amid the two saddles that had belonged to Boyce Lee and Reno.

'Hey, Salty. We gonna leave these saddles on here?' Josh asked the older man.

Turning his head and running a long tongue across his white whiskers, Sagebrush looked at the saddles.

'Toss one down for Tahoka,' he ordered.

'What about the other one?' Willis queried.

Sagebrush's eyes sparkled. 'That one will buy us a lot of drinks when we gets to the Way Station, boy. An awful lotta drinks.'

Watching Tahoka carrying the saddle to his gelding, Zococa paused as the two scouts made room for the beautiful female inside the stagecoach.

The Mexican bandit kissed Clara King's small hand and helped her up into the coach before closing the door as Josh Willis climbed on to his seat next to Sagebrush.

'I have not thanked you properly for saving my life and my blushes, Zococa,' Clara said softly looking down into his handsome features.

Zococa shrugged with uncharacteristic modesty. 'I did nothing and your radiant smile is thanks enough, my lovely one.'

'But I owe you my very life.'

'*Sí*, that is true.' Zococa smiled broadly.

Before she could say anything else, Zococa signalled to Sagebrush on his high seat. The old driver lashed his heavy reins down across the backs of the three remaining horses. The stagecoach rolled through the archway out into the desert.

Tahoka secured his new saddle and led both their mounts out into the sunlight. He mounted his gelding and rubbed his empty stomach thoughtfully.

Zococa was just about to put his boot into his stirrup and mount his pinto stallion, when his keen eyes spotted his own saddle bags lying on the ground next to the empty strongbox beside the stable entrance.

He had quite forgotten filling both satchels of his bags with the valuable coins from the box.

Zococa wrapped his reins around his saddle horn and walked across to the bulging bags. 'I think God is very kind to us, my little elephant.'

Tahoka shrugged and watched his partner picking up the heavy bags before returning to his pinto and placing it behind his saddle cantle. The large Indian used his hands to ask what his partner meant.

'Are you hungry, *amigo?*' Zococa stepped into his stirrup and mounted the stallion. Smiling at his friend, the handsome bandit patted the saddle bags behind him. 'I think you are going to get very fat.'

The two riders rode through the archway out on to the silent desert and aimed their horses south.

'I think we both going to get very fat, little one!' Zococa roared with laughter as they began to increase their pace.